Beyond Vengeance

A Tale of Obsession and Deception

By

Norman Hubley

PublishAmerica
Baltimore

First printing

Hardcover 978-1-4489-3179-8
Softcover 978-1-4489-5218-2
PUBLISHED BY PUBLISHAMERICA, LLLP
www.publishamerica.com
Baltimore

Printed in the United States of America

Author's Note

The text of this book contains a number of typographical errors by the publisher's printer. While none of the errors affect the basic story, I apologize to the reader for their presence.

N. H.

Norman Ashley

DEDICATION

To Annie
my wife for 39 years
who was so much a part of
the creation and my writing
of this story
&
To "Chicki"
my life partner for 18 years now
who was so much a part of
my getting it published
for others to enjoy

ACKNOWLEDGMENTS

I am profoundly grateful to each and every one of the many people who unselfishly gave me their help and support while I was writing this story. They are too numerous for me to set forth here. The following are but a few examples: my law partner Jack Lahive, for his inspiration and encouragement at the very beginning; my Jewish friend, Harold Lavien, for his help with the Judaic aspects of the story; my Dutch friends Berth and Tiny Fruitema, for taking me to and explaining places and things in Amsterdam I wanted to write about; my high school French teacher Anne Hey, for translating my many exchanges of letters with the French Military at the Chateau de Vincennes in France; my friend Eda Rabinovitz, for the Hebrew writing at the beginning of the book; and with special gratitude, my secretary for 32 years Pat Smiley, who shared all my disappointments with rejections and never lost faith in the story or in me.

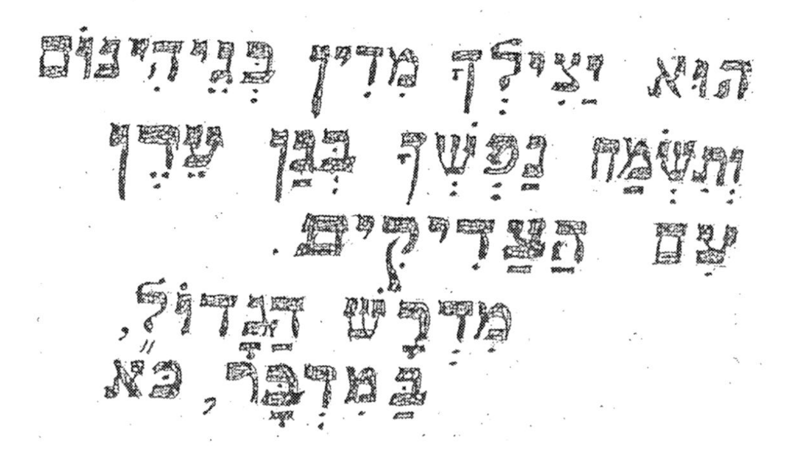

He will deliver thee from judgment in Gehenna, and thy soul will rejoice in Paradise with the righteous..."—Midrash HaGadol Numbers, Ms, 81a

Simserhof

The site had been carefully chosen, the tall trees had been felled and hauled away leaving a clearing less than an acre, surrounded for miles by nothing but the dense woods of Alsace Lorraine. The distance to the German border was just a few meters beyond the reach of France's heaviest artillery piece.

In the center of the clearing, a bundled up construction worker sat poised on the cold metal seat of his yellow bulldozer, rubbing the morning chill out of his arms as he waited for the signal. His machine had been idling for several minutes and the heat from the engine felt good on his legs.

Along the edge of the clearing were more bulldozers, steam shovels and other heavy ground moving machines. Construction workers from every department in France were huddled around them. Everyone's eyes were fixed on the far side of the clearing where a giant of a man dressed in the formal attire of a public official but badly crippled and supporting himself on steel crutches, was talking to a group of military officers. He was France's Minister of Defense. He ended his conversation with the officers, borrowed a pistol from one of them, and hobbled painfully a few steps out into the clearing. He raised the pistol over his head and fired into the air. The shot crackled through the surrounding forest.

The yellow bulldozer in the middle of the clearing lowered its heavy triangular blade. It coughed gray exhaust into the crisp December air as it lumbered forward. The blade's sharp edge plowed through the frozen ground a short distance and then stopped. Everyone cheered. Someone shouted "Vive La France!" The military officers all shook hands.

The furrow made by the bulldozer was less than four meters. An infinitesimal scratch on the soil of France, it marked the beginning of an extraordinary undertaking, one upon which France would stake billions of her francs—and ultimately the freedom of all her soil.

Over the next six years, thousands of contractors, engineers, designers and advisors from the French army and navy would be drawn to the site. Working under a heavy cloak of secrecy, they would construct there, on France's easternmost border, an enormous concrete fortress. It would be large enough to garrison more than a thousand men, with barracks, officers' quarters, command posts, communication centers, recreational areas, kitchens, mess halls, a fully equipped hospital, even a depot for the dead. It would be a fortress with vast storage areas for munitions and supplies, huge generators the size of locomotives to provide power and ventilation, and miles of tunnels and passageways laced with railroad tracks over which troops and ammunition could move quickly from one section to another. It would be unlike any fortress ever built before. It would be a fortress built, except for its gun turrets, entirely inside a mountain.

It would be the first. Others like it would be built inside other mountains at strategic points along the German border. Together, they would form the key links in a complex chain of fortifications that would come to be known as the Maginot Line.

In the spring of 1935, the last of the huge fortresses was completed. Given the name Simserhof, it was fully garrisoned, and lay waiting with its sister fortresses for France's perennial enemy from the east to come within its reach. In May 1940, the enemy came, but not to Simserhof. The German panzers struck in the north, at Sedan. In a matter of weeks, it was all over; France capitulated. Simserhof, its guns never tested, was ordered to surrender ignominiously to a small detachment of German soldiers on motorcycles.

In 1942, Simerserhof was converted into a prison for captured Russians, and placed under the command of a German officer, ironically an Alsatian. For a brief period, a portion was used by the Gestapo for the detention and interrogation of French Jews on their way to concentration camps and extermination. The Germans abandoned the fortress in 1944.

Since the end of World War II, Simserhof has remained under the control of the French military, which has preserved it intact. All vestiges of its having been a prison for Russians or Jews have been removed.

Some days, if the tide is high and there is an east wind, the morning commuters coming up from the subway on Boston's State Street get a special treat: a salt sea smell in the air being blown in off the ocean. Today, they were getting a different treat. It was the first day the temperature had risen above freezing since the beginning of February when the worse winter in thirty years had dumped a record mountain of snow on the city. Even now, the snow was still everywhere, dirty piles of it covering the sidewalks and making the commuters trudge to work in the streets. But for the first time in what seemed an interminable winter, the unmistakable signs were there: the snow was melting; the dirty piles were shrinking; and beneath them there was the sound of water gurgling into the catch basins. It was March now; the sun was higher and sticking around longer. Winter, at last, was calling it quits.

To Mason, winter was a pain in the ass, a long season of inconvenience, the weather just one more variable he had to worry about in arranging meetings with clients and witnesses, and getting briefs filed in court on time. He came up from the subway and sniffed the air. No salt sea smell; the wind was out of the southwest. He crossed State Street and headed dOwn Devonshire, staying in the middle of the street to avoid the deep puddles that reached out from the melting snow banks on both sides. He was still puzzled about the call he got last night from Alex Templeton, the firm's senior partner. The conversation had been brief; all Templeton would say was that he wanted to see Mason this morning about a new matter that would require his working out of the Paris Office for a while. Mason had never been to the Paris Office, or to anywhere in Europe for that matter. Wait a minute, that wasn't quite true, he thought; he was born there, in Metz, France. But he was only a baby when the war broke out. Then his father was killed and his mother fled with him to the United States. She died only a few years later and he was put in a foster home with a family named Mason. The Masons, who had no children, adopted him. He couldn't remember his natural mother at all. Her name was LaBouille, Marie LaBouille, but that was all he knew about her. Funny, he thought, he never had any desire at all to go back to Europe. Even now, he wished Templeton's new matter, whatever it was, would be taking him the other way, to the Far East where he had been in the service. He smiled to himself remembering the two years he spent out there. The Viet Nam War hadn't heated up yet. He was sent to Okinawa and stationed at a large military base that had its own football, baseball, and basketball teams. He wasn't good enough to make any of them, so tried out for a judo team it also had there.

He didn't know anything about judo, but tried out for the team anyway, and made it. He found he liked the sport. It got rough at times but didn't have any of the hitting or kicking of Karate; it was all throwing techniques where timing and off-balancing were the key, and you could beat the other guy without injuring him. He also found that he had a flair for the sport. He worked his way up to black belt and spent the rest of his two years traveling all over southeast Asia, competing in judo contests and generally enjoying himself.

He continued to think about his judo as he made his way down Devonshire. *Uchi Mata,* that was his throw. He had won a lot of matches with the old inner thigh throw that was just made for tall guys like him with long legs. You had to move the other guy around the mat a little first and get him to spread his feet. Then, when he shifts his weight from one foot to the other, you yank him towards you, spin in fast and low, and sweep your leg back up in an arabesque, catching him hard on his inner thigh. You don't even feel the guy fly upside down over your shoulder.

Mason reached the end of Devonshire and stopped. In front of him, at the corner of Milk Street, a huge puddle had flooded out into the intersection. He waited at the edge of it for several cars to go by. Going to Paris would mean giving up his weekly workouts at the Kodokan Club where he still did some judo to stay in shape. That was something he was going to miss. Oh well, he thought, he was getting too old for the sport now anyway. He wasn't as fast as he used to be; the young black belts were all getting tougher to deal with. He waited for what he thought was the last car to go by, and then started out into the intersection. He had only taken a step or two when he saw another car was corning It was an old beat up Chevrolet, its windshield covered with snow. It was coming right at him and was going to hit him if he didn't get out of the way. He jumped back and landed with a splash in the middle of the big puddle. He looked down at the cold water pouring in over his rubbers. He climbed up on the snow bank and stood there for a moment. He shook his head. "Jesus! What a way to start the week.

* * *

The old grandfather's clock that had stood in the reception area of Whitaker, Brown, Thorndike and Templeton since the firm was founded in 1927 was just striking nine when Mason arrived. The young receptionist looked up at him and smiled. "Good morning, Mr. Mason."

"Hi, Jean. The old man in yet?"

"No, not yet."

"Do me a favor, will you?"

"Sure. What?"

"As soon as he comes in, give me a call and let me know." "Okay." She made a note on her pad.

Mason crossed the reception area and walked down the main corridor to his office. His secretary was already busy typing. She interrupted what she was doing to hand him a pink message slip. "Mr. Templeton's secretary called to remind you of your meeting with him his morning."

Mason took the pink slip. "Thanks. And do me a favor; get me a bunch of paper towels." He walked into his office, picked up the morning mail on his desk and glanced through it. It was the same old stuff: three letters from opposing lawyers about extensions of time, two asking for his consent, one consenting to a request he had made; a memorandum of law he had asked an associate to prepare; several interoffice memos; and the usual brochures describing trial practice seminars in Miami, Las Vegas and other places picked by the Bar Association to encourage attendance. There was nothing that demanded his immediate attention. He took off his coat and hung it up. His secretary appeared with the paper towels. He took them, walked behind his desk, and spread them out on the floor around his chair. He sat down, took off his shoes and put them upside down on the radiator. Then, holding one foot at a time over the wastebasket, he peeled off his sopping wet socks, wrung them out, and placed them next to his shoes. He swung around and planted his bare feet on the paper towels.

The telephone rang. It was the receptionist. "Mr. Templeton just came in."

"Thanks." Mason hung up. He pushed the button on his desk that made his secretary appear. "Mary, skip my coffee this morning; I'll have it with Templeton." He handed her the pile of papers on his desk. "And take care of these, will you? Write Stone and Hagen; tell them I agree to the extensions they want. Write a short note to Ruggio thanking him for agreeing to the one I requested. File the memos and throw the rest of this crap away."

The telephone rang again. This time it was Templeton's secretary. "Mr. Mason, Mr_ Templeton is ready to meet with you whenever you can come around to his office."

"Okay, I'll be right there." Mason reached over and felt one of the socks on the radiator. It was still soaking wet.

* * *

Alexander Templeton, in his late seventies, was the only one of the firm's founders still alive. More than just the titular head of the firm, he still had an active practice that brought him into the office every day. Although he now referred most of his practice to his younger partners, his continued presence in the firm was assurance to his clients that any matter he took on for them would meet the high standards for which Whitaker, Brown, Thorndike and Templeton had always been noted. Templeton was childless and now a widower. His wife, to whom he was devoted, had died two years ago. He now had only four interests in life; golf, to which he had become addicted recently and played poorly; bridge which he studied and played well; the practice of law; and above all the continued well being of the firm he had founded. Over the years, he had seen it grow to a size he had never contemplated and become one of the largest and most prestigious in Boston. Now, with his wife gone, it was his only real love. A first rate lawyer but also a practical businessman, he had that rare sense of balance between what was right and what was reasonable. Despite his age, he was still regarded by all his partners as the head of the firm. He was chairman of its Managing Committee, its Compensation Committee, and its New Clients Committee.

It was in this last capacity that he was meeting this morning with his young partner, Steve Mason. He pressed the buzzer on the side of his desk and waited for his secretary to appear.

"Yes, Mr. Templeton?"

"Did you reach Mr. Mason?"

"Yes, he's coming right around."

"When he arrives, bring in some coffee for him. I'll have my usual tea. Then hold all my calls; I don't want us to be disturbed."

As she left, Mason entered. Templeton stood up and shook his hand. "Good morning, Steve, it was nice of you to find time to meet with me on such short notice." He motioned Mason to one of the red leather chairs in front of this desk. "How have you been? I haven't seen much of you since you tried that Dalton case for me. I'm sure I told you how delighted the client was with the result."

Mason nodded. "You did, yes. That was a tough case, but we got a few breaks."

Templeton's secretary appeared with the coffee and tea on a silver tray. She placed it on the desk, and then slipped out of the office quietly, closing the door behind her.

Templeton lifted the teabag out of his cup, then lowered it back in again. He looked across his desk at Mason. "Steve, does 'Gezar Kopt' mean anything to you?"

Mason shook his head. "No, what is it?"

Templeton leaned back and laughed. "It's a person; it's a man's name, 'Gezar Kopt.' He's an Israeli."

"Never heard of him."

"Well, he's the reason I wanted to meet with you this morning." Templeton lifted the tea bag out of his cup and placed it on the saucer. "He's the new client I mentioned last night. We've done a few small things for him already. He looks like he could be a major source of new business for the firm. He's the head of a large international conglomerate that owns a number of very profitable companies in Europe. Until recently, his operations have been exclusively over there. He has decided to expand into the United States and is looking for a major law firm to represent him over here. He anticipates generating a substantial amount of legal business for the firm he ultimately chooses."

Mason drank some of his coffee. "Sounds like a nice client to get." Templeton nodded. "Yes, but there's something strange about him" "He wouldn't be the first strange client we've had."

Templeton smiled. "No, that's for sure. Still, this fellow is different somehow; his strangeness has an elusive quality about it."

"How so?"

"Well, it's more a feeling I have than anything concrete. As far as we can detelinine, he seems legitimate enough."

"What's his background; do we know that?"

Templeton shook his head. "We have been able to learn very little about him. We know that back in the fifties, when Jews all over the world were trying to help out the new state of Israel by investing money there, Kopt was the principal broker they would deal with. Later on, when the situation reversed and Israeli money was flowing out of the country for investment elsewhere, it was Kopt who—"

"—Who had the inside track again."

"Exactly."

Mason smiled. "So he made a killing both ways, when the money came in, and again when it went out."

Templeton nodded. "That's one way of putting it, yes."

"You said we've already done a few small things for him. How did they work out?"

"Fine, fine." Templeton took a sip of his tea. "But still, there was something odd about them all the same."

"In what way?"

"Well, first I should say that he pays well. He insists on paying our top rate for everything. And he pays right away, as soon as he gets our bill."
"We certainly can't knock that."

"No, that's right. So far, we've handled three different matters for him. The first one involved setting up a new subsidiary corporation here in the United States to be held jointly by two of his European companies. Because the transaction had significant tax implications, I decided that, in addition to our corporate people, someone from our tax department should also attend the closing. I mentioned this to Kopt and was surprised when he told me he did not want anyone from our office to attend the closing."

"You mean anyone from the tax department."

"No. I mean anyone, not even from our corporate department." "Did he say who was going to handle the closing?"

Templeton shook his head. "No. He just said he had engaged us simply to prepare the papers, that we had done all he wanted, and that he was entirely satisfied."

"That's all?"

"Well, I did argue with him a bit. I explained it was normal practice in the United States for the lawyers who prepare the papers also attend the closing. I said that if other lawyers were going to handle it, our people should at least be present to answer any questions that might arise. I even offered to have our corporate and tax people attend the closing at our expense."

"What did he say to that?"

"He thanked me for my offer but was adamant that no one from our office was necessary." Templeton leaned forward over his desk. "And get this part, Steve: he said he was perfectly willing to pay whatever additional fee would have been involved if they were to attend."

"That is strange!"

"Another matter he asked us to handle required our sending Bill Chapman of our labor department to Israel for a series of meetings with the director of one of Kopt's companies there. Chapman came back puzzled why he had been sent. He said he was treated royally, learned a lot about Israel's history, but never once was asked to do anything and might just as well stayed home. He said he felt guilty billing the client for the time he spent over there. The other thing Kopt asked us to do was some legal research on an obscure point of law involving the doctrine of *ronvoir* between Israel and France. I told him the question was one he would be better advised to have researched by a French or Israeli lawyer but he insisted we do it."

Mason nodded. "I have to agree this guy Kopt sounds a bit odd." He put his empty coffee cup back on the silver tray. "But how do I fit into all this?"

Templeton got up from his desk and walked to the window. "He has come to us with another matter."

"And?"

"He wants you to handle it."

Mason was surprised. "You mean he asked for me specifically?" "Not exactly. But in a way, yes."

"I don't understand."

"Let me explain. A few days ago, he came to see me again. He said another matter has arisen in which we might be of assistance. He said it was a matter or the utmost delicacy and there were three conditions we would have to meet if we took it on. The first one was easy; he said the matter would have to be handled out of our Paris Office. I told him this was certainly no problem. The second was more complicated and a bit puzzling. He said the matter required a particular type of lawyer."

"Did you ask him what particular type he had in mind?"

"No. I just let him go on; I knew he would tell me."

"Which he did?"

"Yes. He said it had to be a lawyer who at sometime in the past had lived in France. He said it was not important when, or for how long he had lived there, but he had to have actually lived there, not simply been there as a tourist or on business. I told him the four lawyers we have assigned to the Paris Office all met this requirement, and I was certain there were others in the firm who also did. He said he wanted to see a list of the people and was adamant that the list not omit anyone who might possibly qualify." Templeton looked at Mason and smiled. "I almost left you off the list, Steve; then I remembered that you were born there."

Mason laughed. "Wow! That's drawing a long bow! I was born there, yes, in Metz, on May 10, 1940, the same day the Germans invaded. But hell, I was still only a baby when my mother fled the country and brought me over here. Then she died about a year or so later. I don't even remember her."

"What about your father?"

"I never knew anything about him."

Templeton reached into the drawer of his desk and took out two large cigars. He offered one to Mason.

Mason shook his head. "No, thanks. But I'd like to have a little more coffee, just to warm up a bit."

Templeton pressed the buzzer on his desk. His secretary appeared. "Bring Mr. Mason some more coffee. And turn the heat up a little in here for us." He put one of the cigars back in the drawer, took out a heavy silver lighter, and lit the one he had kept for himself. He took several puffs, and then continued. "I agree, Steve, that putting your name on the list was drawing a long bow. But Kopt was emphatic that he wanted me to list everyone who had lived in Franc at any time and technically you had lived there. I figured that when he read your resume and saw the situation in your case, he'd simply eliminate you. Some of the others on the list, Steiner, Williams, and of course Marion Fornier, who studied at the Sorbonne, all lived in France for significant periods of time. I was betting he would pick on of them." Templeton paused to puff again on his cigar. "Yesterday afternoon, Kopt called me. He said he had considered all the people on the list I had given him, and—"

Mason finished the sentence for him. "—And had picked me." "Yes, and had picked you."

"Did he say why?"

"No."

"So, what's the job he wants us to do?"

"We don't know."

Mason frowned. "We don't know?"

"That's the third condition. If we take on the job, you're the only one who is to know what it is, no one else."

"You mean not even in the firm?"

"That's right, not even me. Kopt was quite specific about that. He assured me it did not involve anything illegal or unethical. But he was adamant we had to agree you'd be the only one to know."

Mason took a sip of the second cup of coffee. He sat back in his chair. "Maybe this time, we should tell him to go to hell."

Templeton blew a cloud of cigar smoke up at the ceiling. "There's something else Kopt said that I think we have to consider. He said if we take on this job, he will retain our firm as his legal counsel for all his matters here in the United States. He said substantial legal services will be required and he is prepared to pay us an annual retainer of five million dollars."

For a few minutes, neither of them said anything. Templeton puffed on his cigar. Mason took several more sips of his coffee, and then broke the silence. "That's a lot of money."

Templeton nodded. "Yes it is, Steve. We have to think twice before turning away business like that. I've discussed the whole matter with the Managing Committee. We all feel that, unless Kopt wants us to do something illegal or unethical, we should try to do it."

Mason thought for a moment. "Well, I guess there's not much point in trying to decide whether we can take the matter on or not until we know what it is."

Templeton smiled. "Until you know what it is, you mean."

Mason smiled back. "That's right; until I know what it is."

Templeton stood up, walked around his desk and put his hand on Mason's shoulder. "Steve, this fellow Kopt is an odd duck. I still have an uncomfortable feeling about him. When you find out what it is he wants us to do, if there's anything that makes you think we shouldn't take it on, then..." He paused. "—the firm will understand. But if we can possibly do it, I mean unless there's some good reason for not doing it, I'd like to see the firm get this account, and not have it go elsewhere." He patted Mason on the shoulder. "I realize I'm putting you on the spot, Steve, but I know I can count on your judgment. If you decide we can do what Kopt wants, let's do it. If you decide otherwise, well, as I said...the firm will understand."

Mason looked at him. "Well, I suppose the next step is for me to find how what the hell he has in mind."

"He wants you to meet him today at noon. He's staying at the Ritz and wants you to come up there."

"The Ritz, huh? Did he say why he wanted to meet there and not here at the office?"

"No."

Mason shrugged. "Okay, so it's the Ritz; I'll go there. Anything else we should talk about on this?"

"No, I've told you everything I know."

Mason got up and walked to the door. He opened it, and then paused. "Well, I suppose you should wish me luck."

Templeton smiled.do wish you luck, Steve. And I know you'll make the right decision." As Mason started to leave, Templeton stopped him.

"Oh, one other thing."

"What?"

Templeton pointed to Mason's feet. "I think, if you're going over to the Ritz, Steve, you probably want to put on your socks."

* * *

The snow had been removed from the sidewalk in front of the Ritz. Mason climbed out of the taxi and walked into the hotel's lobby. He unbuttoned his overcoat and took off his scarf while he waited for the clerk at the reception desk to finish talking on the telephone. The clerk hung up. "Yes sir, what can I do for you?"

"I'm here to see one of your guests, a Mr. Kopt, that's K 0 P T. The clerk ran his finger down the list of names in the register. "Oh, yes, Mr. Kopt; he's staying in 709, one of our parlor suites."

"Thanks."

Mason took the elevator to the seventh floor and followed the room numbers to the end of the hall. On the last door, below the number 709, was a small white button. He pressed it and waited. He was about to press it again when he heard someone coming to the door.

"Who is it?"

"It's Steve Mason."

The door opened. "Ah, Mr. Mason! Please come in. I'm Gezar Kopt." He shook Mason's hand.

Mason's first impression of Kopt was that of a Minotaur in reverse: a man with the body of a bull. He was in his early fifties, short and heavy, with a thick neck, massive shoulders and, beneath his expensive tailored suit, what Mason could tell was a solid muscular body capable of great physical strength. His head, almost completely bald, was large and out of proportion to the rest of him. His eyes and nose seemed small and crowded together in the middle of his round hairless face. An almost indiscernible chin was buried in flabby jowls that hung over the stiff white collar of his shirt. He pointed to a closet where Mason could hang his overcoat, then turned and walked back into the center of the room. There was something wrong with his right leg. He had a pronounced limp, each step requiring him to lean heavily on a thick, ivory-knobbed cane. He turned and smiled at Mason. "Come, come, Mr. Mason, you do not have to stand there by the closet. Come over here and make yourself comfortable." He motioned with his cane for Mason to sit in one of the soft chairs. "You know, I enjoy staying here at the Ritz; it is not plush, but quite satisfactory."

"It's generally regarded as the best we have in Boston."

"I have stayed in more elegant places, of course, but I like it here all the same; the service is good and the hotel is quiet."

As Mason sat down he glanced around Kopt's suite. The door to the bedroom was open but the room was dark. The shades were drawn and the only light was coming from a television set, the sound from which was barely audible. Kopt saw the bedroom had caught Mason's attention. "I'm afraid that is another of my idiosyncrasies; I like to watch television in the dark." He paused and smiled. I imagine your senior partner, Alex Templeton, has already told you about my being given to certain idiosyncrasies."

Mason settled back in the chair. "He mentioned that some of the things you did were a bit out of the ordinary."

Kopt laughed. "Ah, spoken like a true lawyer!"

For a few moments, neither of them said anything. Then Kopt broke the silence. "I thought we might have a light lunch while we talk." He took a room service menu from one of the tables and handed it to Mason. "Here, look this over and let me know what you would like. Then I will tell you what the assignment I have in mind for you is all about."

Mason glanced at the menu. "A turkey club and a Heineken will be fine."

Kopt sat down on the sofa, picked up the telephone, and dialed room service. For the first time, his eyes left Mason. Mason felt relieved. Kopt's eyes had a strange penetrating quality about them. Mason was certain he had never met Kopt before; yet Kopt seemed to be studying him, as if trying to remember him from somewhere.

Kopt reached room service, gave them Mason's order, and added a glass of warm milk for himself. He hung up and smiled at Mason. "1 envy your being able to eat what you want. My stomach was, you might say, one of the casualties of the war. When I say the war, I mean World War II. But of course you are too young to remember that."

"I was only five years old when it was over."

"Of course, of course. Actually, I was only a young man myself. I was twelve when it started and eighteen when it ended. You might be interested in where I spent the last three years of the war." He paused. "A place called Mauthausen."

"Wasn't that one of those—?"

"Yes, a concentration camp."

"I thought so, one of those places like Auschwitz and Dachau."

"Yes." Kopt smiled. This time there was something different about his smile. He leaned forward, resting both hands on the ivory knob of his cane. "I would like to tell you about Mauthausen."

Mason could see that Kopt was clearly studying him now. He sat back in his chair and let him continue.

"I was only a boy, barely fifteen when I was sent to Mauthausen. The Germans had killed my father and mother, and I was sent there along with the other Jews from my village. I was there only a few weeks when something happened that, as it turned out, saved my life. Each day at noon, we were lined up, several hundred of us, to be fed. We were fed only once a day and it was always the same thing: potato soup, just a watery broth made from potato skins But it was all we would get until the next day. We were each given a small wooden bowl, then herded in single file past the big iron kettles that had the soup in them. Most of the time, there was barely enough soup to feed us all. This particular day, however, the Germans had miscalculated and after all of us had received a bowl of soup, there was a little left over. The guards, seeing the extra soup, did a foolish thing. They just walked away from the kettles, announcing that anyone who wanted more could have it. Everyone—" Kopt interrupted himself. "Oh, forgive me, I should have asked you this before; would you like to have a drink while we are waiting for lunch to arrive? I have some whiskey, or sherry if you prefer?"

"No, thanks, I'll wait for the Heineken."

Kopt resumed his narrative. "As I started to say, everyone, still hungry, rushed back. The first ones back to the kettles plunged their arms down inside them to fill their bowls again. Others rushed up and squeezed beside them. More kept coming, crowding in, trying to get their bowls into the kettles. People began pushing and shoving one another. I started to go, but stopped. I could see it was becoming a melee. I decided it was not worth it. I sat down and contented myself with licking my bowl again. The trouble at the kettles got worse; people began fighting, hitting each other with their fists. The Germans stepped in and started clubbing everyone with the butts of their rifles: old men, women, children, everyone. People were screaming and falling to the ground bleeding. It was horrible. The next morning I was summoned to the Commandant's office. He was sitting behind his desk, and as I stood at attention in front of him, I did not know what to expect. He said he had heard what I had done the day before, how I had stayed out of the trouble over the extra soup. He said it showed good sense on my part. The upshot was that he assigned me to work in his office, typing. I had typing lessons in school and could type fairly well." Kopt interrupted his narrative to put both hands on the ivory knob of his cane and hoist himself awkwardly up from the sofa. "You will have to forgive me again but sometimes this leg of mine objects if I sit too long without exercising it." He steadied himself and then limped into the center of the room where he began walking back and forth, leaning heavily on the cane. He looked at Mason and smiled. "Where was I?"

"You had just got a job in the Commandant's office."

"Ah, yes. Now it was unusual for a Jew in a concentration camp to have any influence over his German guards. But, because of my job in the Commandant's office, I did have some. And I used it. It was part of my job to type up each day the daily reports the guards had to sign before going off duty. I curried the favor of one guard by always typing his report first. He returned the favor by breaking the rules and giving me one of the heavy blankets only the guards had. That blanket saved my life. It also saved the life of another boy in the camp with whom I had become friends, Otto Rothman. Otto was only twelve. Both of us would have died if we did not have that blanket to keep us warm at night."

Kopt limped back to the sofa and sat down again. "In 1945, shortly before the war ended, Otto and I decided to escape. We were only boys and did not realize the impossible task we were undertaking. We waited until late at night, then crept out of our barracks and along the concrete path by the fence. Inching our way on our stomachs to avoid the sweeping searchlight, we followed the fence to the far end. We waited for the searchlight to pass over us, then quickly scrambled to our feet and climbed up. The fence was not electrified but was heavily barbed. It was a dark night and we could not see where we were going. I had almost reached the top of the fence when I accidentally grabbed one of the sharp barbs. It was like a knife stabbing into my hand, and I felt the pain shoot up my arm. I had to let go and fell back on the concrete, breaking my leg as I landed. I looked up and saw that Otto, too, had grabbed one of the barbs. He had started to fall too, but could not let go; the barb was imbedded in his hand. He kicked frantically, trying to fmd the fence again with his feel, but it was too dark. He was swinging back and forth, the whole weight of his body pulling the sharp barb deeper into his hand. The pain he was suffering was excruciating, but he did not cry out because he knew it would give us away. I could hear him pleading with me Gezar, Gezar, crawl away. You can make it, Gezar.'"

Mason shifted uncomfortably in his chair. "What happened then?"

"The guards came; they had spotted us with the searchlight. When Otto saw them, he began screaming 'Cut me down! Please cut me down!' Then the guards dragged me away."

"What about Otto?"

Kopt took a handkerchief out of his pocket and wiped his forehead where a few beads of sweat had appeared. "They left him hanging there."

Mason winced. "Jesus!"

"They left him there until morning so the other inmates could see him. Then they cut him down. He was still alive but his hand was all but torn off

There was an inmate in the camp who had been a doctor. He did what he could but was only able to save the thumb and small finger."

Mason winced again. "I think I will have that drink after all."

Kopt limped over to a small table on which there were two bottles and some glasses. "Whiskey or sherry?"

"Whiskey."

"How would you like it?"

"Straight. Just straight."

Kopt brought Mason the whiskey. He poured himself a small sherry and then sat down again on the sofa. He continued his story. "Otto and I were certain we would be shot for trying to escape. But the war was then almost over. The Americans had crossed the Rhine and the Russians were at the outskirts of Berlin. The Germans knew it was just a matter of time before they would have to surrender. Only a few days after our attempted escape, the Germans herded everyone together in the center of the camp. They announced that they expected heavy Allied bombing and were going to put us in a large cave near the camp where we would be safe. They opened the gate to the camp and ordered us to start marching Nobody moved; we just stood there. For the first time we refused to do what we were ordered. The Commandant came strutting out of this office and began shouting over the loudspeakers. He said he was putting us in the cave for our own protection. We still refused to move. He said he was ordering us into the cave; if we did not start marching we would be shot. Still we refused. We knew they wanted us to go in the cave so they could gas us and seal the cave up afterwards. The Commandant saw we were not moving. He ordered trucks brought in with machine guns in the back. The trucks turned around so the guns were pointing at us. It was a tense moment. We all stood there, waiting for the Commandant to give the order to fire. I remember closing my eyes. After what seemed an eternity, I opened them again. I saw the Commandant shrug his shoulders and wave the trucks away. Then he ordered us back to work and disappeared into his office. The next day, when we woke up, the Gellnans were gone; they had even taken their dogs. We did not know what to do. All morning we just wandered around the camp. Then, about midday, we saw the first Allied soldier. He was a Canadian." Kopt paused. "It was not long after that when the war ended." He took out his handkerchief again, this time to wipe his eyes.

Mason sat back in his chair. "That's quite a story."

Kopt hoisted himself off the sofa and began walking back and forth again. "Yes, but there is more. After the war, for many of us, things were not much better. We were no longer mistreated as we had been by the Germans, but we still found ourselves herded together in camps and shipped here and there, like cattle, from one place to another. We were wretched, dispossessed Jews; we had nothing and no one wanted us. We were what the newspapers called 'Displaced Persons.' Otto and I decided to leave Europe and go to Israel. It was not called that then; it was still Palestine, governed under mandate by the British. We joined the Irgun and the fight for an independent state of Israel.' He paused. "You have heard of the Irgun?"

Mason nodded. "They were an Israeli guerrilla group that fought against the Arabs and even against the British, if I remember right."

"That's right. But not all of us in the Irgun were involved in the actual fighting. I, myself, was not. I served in a different way. It was a time when Jews everywhere wanted to see Israel win her independence, and were anxious to give money to that end. My job was to create an organization to receive that money and channel it where it was needed most. It may be immodest of me to say so, but I did a good job. The money poured in. At first, in the early days, almost all the money we received was used for arms and ammunition and explosives. Later on, we were able to use some of it to obtain influence with key individuals in the United Nations who were dealing with the Middle East." Kopt smiled. "'Lobbying' is what I believe you call it over here." He stopped walking back and forth and stood leaning on his cane. "Otto, however, was very much involved in the fighting. He was with one of the Irgun's special commando units."

Mason sipped his drink. "He must have been handicapped by the injury he received in the concentration camp."

Kopt began walking back and forth again. "Yes, but he more than compensated for that. During the months we were still in Europe, in the relocation camps, he devoted virtually every waking moment to a regimen for building up his body. He would exercise for hours on end every day. By the time we left for Israel, he was as strong as an ox, and had developed an extraordinary strength and quickness in the arm that had not been injured. He was more than a match for most men with two hands. In the Irgun, he became one of their most feared commandos. The others called him the '*Shcheeta*.'" Kopt smiled. "But, of course, you do not understand Hebrew."

Mason laughed. "Not a word."

Kopt smiled. "'*Shcheeta'* is the Hebrew word for the kosher slaughter. More precisely, it is the stroke of the slaughterer's knife, delivered so swiftly, effectively, and without warning, that death is unexpected and instantaneous." He paused. "The knife, a most underrated weapon, Mr. Mason. Limited, of course, if one's adversary is at a distance. But up close, oh, that is something else again. And when one is a commando, one's adversary is usually quite close. No one was more proficient with the knife than Otto. He was the one who dealt with the sentry. His stroke across the throat was like lightning, severing the larynx before the slightest sound could be uttered. Yes, Otto could—" Kopt was interrupted by a knock at the door. "That must be our lunch." He turned to Mason with an apology. "How stupid of me! Here you are about to have lunch and I am rambling on about gory details of the past. You must forgive me." He limped across the room and opened the door. A waiter in a stiff white jacket entered, pushing a service cart covered with a linen tablecloth. On it were Mason's sandwich and beer, and a tall glass of milk. Kopt waited for the waiter to leave, then sat down again on the sofa. "I should apologize for being so long winded. You must be wondering what all this has to do with why you are here."

Mason shrugged. "It's part of a lawyer's job to listen; I assume what you've been telling me has a bearing on what you want me to do."

Kopt took a sip of his warm milk. "Alex Templeton, I am sure, told you I am a man of some financial means."

"He mentioned it, yes."

"The truth is I am quite wealthy. I have made a great deal of money trading in money. And I have made it all because of Israel. If Israel had not given me the opportunities she did, I would not be where I am today. I owe her a great debt. For that reason, and because of my own experience, I am devoting this time of my life to a cause very important to Israel and close to the hearts of Jews throughout the world."

Mason took a bite of his sandwich. "Which is?"

Kopt's face hardened. "Helping her fmd those responsible for the Holocaust, who are still alive and hiding somewhere."

"You mean like Eichmann?"

"Yes, but of course Eichmann was a special case. When he was found in South America, he was forcibly taken back to Israel to be tried and hanged. His case was handled by a quite different organization; our organization does not do anything like that." When we fmd someone, we simply expose him."

"What do you mean?"

"We reveal his identity to the world, strip him of whatever facade he has been living behind, and let everyone see the guilt he shares for the Holocaust." Kopt leaned forward, his hands grasping the ivory knob of his cane. "What we want you to do, Mr. Mason, is help us fmd one of these people, an ex German officer named Hans Molte. We have already made several attempts to find him, but they have all failed. He has proven particularly elusive. We know he is alive and living somewhere in Europe."

"But you don't know where."

"No. We do know, however, that he has a daughter in Paris who has changed her name to Helms, Lisa Helms She is not his real daughter; her parents were killed in the war. But Molte raised her from the time she was a little girl and she thinks of him as her father. She communicates with him regularly, even visits him from time to time."

"I assume you've had her followed."

Kopt nodded. "Yes, we have tried several times to get her to lead us to him but without success. She is a clever woman and is now on to us. We have to try something different."

Mason smiled. "And that's where I come in."

Kopt fmished his milk and wiped the corners of his mouth with his napkin. "Yes, Mr. Mason, that is where you come in. We want you to go to Paris and arrange somehow to meet her, make friends with her, and gain her confidence."

"And then get her to tell me where her father is."

Kopt nodded. "Yes."

"And then—?"

"That's all."

"That's all?"

"Once we know where Molte is, we will do the rest"

Mason had finished his sandwich and beer. He stood up and walked to the window. Outside, the day was bright and sunny, the sun melting the snow everywhere. He stood there for a few moments watching the water drip off the pitched roof across the street. Then he turned and looked at Kopt. "Why me?"

Kopt smiled. "You mean, why did we pick you for the job?"

"Yes. It doesn't exactly strike me as a job for a trial lawyer."

Kopt broke into a broad smile and pounded his heavy cane on the floor. "Precisely! That is precisely why we picked you. Frauline Helms knows we will never give up trying to find her father; that sooner or later we will be sending someone else to try again. But a trial lawyer from Boston, who is not Jewish, and who has never had any connection with Israel—even as on guard as she is, she will not suspect you, particularly with the cover story we have provided for you." He paused and smiled. "You may also have wondered why I told Alex Templeton I wanted someone who had lived in Europe."

Mason nodded. "The question did cross my mind "

"The explanation may seem strange to you, not being a Jew. It only makes sense, perhaps, if one is a Jew who has lived through the Holocaust. In our organization, we are all such Jews. We believe that the instrument of our work in a matter such as this should be someone who lived, or, in your case, whose parents lived in Europe and suffered because of the Nazis." He paused and smiled. "But it is not necessary that you understand all of this "You can simply chalk it up as another of my idiosyncrasies."

Mason shrugged. "You were starting to say something about a cover story I would have."

"Ah yes, the cover story." Kopt reached down and picked up a manila folder full of papers he had placed on the floor beside the sofa. "It's all in here." He handed the folder to Mason. "The story is complicated but has been carefully prepared and is totally believable. You are to study everything in there until you have memorized it and are letter perfect, then you are to destroy it. The information is to be in your head, nowhere else. You will, of course, need time to study it all. For now, I will simply summarize it."

Mason settled back in his chair. "Okay, go ahead."

Kopt leaned forward. "Well, to begin with, your law firm is sending you to Europe to work on a new matter that has come into its Paris Office. It is a litigation matter, which is why you were chosen to handle it. The new client is a German company Chemisches Hoch Frieren Gesekkschaft." He smiled. "I will refer to it simply as 'Hoch.' It is a large chemical company specializing in industrial processes using chemicals with high freezing points. One of its principal products is a process that allows high freezing point chemicals to be used without the usual and expensive warming systems like steam tracing and thermal jacketing of pipes." Kopt pointed to the folder Mason was holding. "The technical details are all in there; I will not go into them. The reason Hoch has consulted your firm is that a French company, Compagnie Chimique Industrelle, has begun marketing a competitive product, claiming it can do everything Hoch's can. Chimique's process is less expensive because, although their advertising does not say so, it still requires some tracing or jacketing. Hoch, which intends to file a law suit against Chimique, is already feeling the affects of the competition and is being forced to close some of its sales offices." Kopt paused to pull himself up again from the sofa and limp out into the middle of the room. "Hoch knows that when the sales offices are closed, the managers of them will be unhappy. It also knows it will need these sales managers as witnesses in the lawsuit again Chemique. Hoch has asked your Paris Office to prepare the lawsuit and to obtain affidavits from all of them before they learn their offices are to be closed."

Mason had a question. "This company, Hoch, is it—?"

"—A real company? Yes. It is one of my subsidiaries in Germany. Actually it has the process I described and is concerned about competition from Chimique. But the matter is unlikely ever to go so far as a lawsuit. However, this is unimportant; I have arranged things so that everyone at Hoch is convinced a lawsuit is imminent. The company engineer who will assist you on the case is quite excited about suing Chimique; he is absolutely outraged at what they are doing."

"So, even he doesn't know it's a cover story."

Kopt shook his large head. “No, no one except you will know that. The engineer has been instructed to help you with technical details but otherwise leave all aspects of the matter to you. He has been told that, as a lawyer, you will know what the affidavits must contain to be useful in court if the sales managers decide to testify against Hoch.” Kopt pointed again at the folder, which Mason had now put in his lap. “Also in there is a narrative of the personal background we want you to have. By and large, your real background is satisfactory. However, we thought it wise to make a few embellishments.” He paused. “Do you remember your grandfather, Austin Mason?”

Mason was surprised. “Sure. I was only a kid when he died, but I remember him. He was a trainman on the old New York, New Haven and Hartford Railroad. He used to let me sit on his lap and wind his big pocket watch; I remember that.”

Kopt smiled. “Well, we have posthumously made him very wealthy man.”

Mason laughed. “That’s a switch. He was a nice guy, but he certainly wasn’t wealthy.”

Kopt continued with the cover story. “Back in the twenties, your kindly old grandfather was deeply involved in that ambivalently regarded activity you Americans call ‘bootlegging.’ When Prohibition ended, he converted his operation into a legitimate liquor distributorship and went on to make millions. Before he died, he set up trust funds for his grandchildren. You were his favorite, and the fund set up for you was the largest. It does not become available to you until next year, but then you will receive several million dollars.”

Mason laughed. “I wish this weren’t a cover story.”

Kopt went on. “In anticipation of your inheritance, the Chase Manhattan Bank in New York has given you a letter of credit against which you can draw sizable amounts of money.” He paused. “I have arranged with the Chase to give you such a letter so you can actually draw these amounts.”

“Which are?”

“Up to thirty thousand dollars a month.”

Mason’s eyes widened. “That’s a lot of money.”

"We want you to have a lot of money. We want you to draw as much as you need, and to spend it freely but not recklessly. Frauline Helms is a woman, and women fmd something exciting about men who have money and know how to spend it. We want her to see you as someone who has a great deal of family wealth but is not spoiled by it." He pointed again to the folder. "There is nothing in there to tell you how to create that impression; that is something you will have to carry off on your own. I have made arrangements with the Chase so that if you have anything to report to me, you are to send a telex to a Mr. Arthur Sawyer there. He has been instructed to forward it directly to me. You should, however, be discreet in what you say. If I want to communicate with you, I will do so through Sawyer."

Mason nodded. "I understand."

Kopt smiled. "Now, I suppose, you would like to know something about Fraulein Helms."

"Everything you can tell me."

Kopt pointed to the folder. "There are some photographs of her in there, all taken, of course, without her knowledge."

Mason poked through the folder and found the photographs. He looked at them one by one. Lisa Helms was certainly beautiful. In the first one, she was in a museum looking thoughtfully at a small sculpture on a pedestal. Tall, with long blond hair that fell evenly over her shoulders, she had a face that was a perfect oval, high cheekbones and deep almond shaped eyes. Her mouth, wide and sensual, was drawn into a perplexed pout as she studied the *objet d'art* in front of her. She was dressed casually in an open, loose fitting jacket, turtleneck sweater and jeans.

Kopt pointed to the photograph. "That was taken in the Louve just a few months ago. She spends quite a bit of her time there. She is interested in art, particularly sculpture. She does some sculpturing herself as a hobby. The next one was taken at a restaurant called 'Au Pied de Couchon' in the old Les Halles section of Paris. It is one of her favorites; she has dinner there quite often."

Mason looked at the next photograph and smiled. It showed Lisa caught in that awkward moment when, with too much food on her fork, she was struggling to get it all in her mouth at the same time. Even in such an unguarded moment, she was beautiful, Mason thought. He turned to Kopt. "How often does she go to this restaurant, the—?"

"—Au Pied de Couchon. At least one a week when she is in Paris."

Mason looked at the rest of the photographs. In one, Lisa was standing on the sidewalk in the rain waving frantically for a taxi. Another showed her coming out of a bakery, the ubiquitous loaf of French bread under her arm. In another, she was sitting curled up on a park bench, her shoes off, reading a book and eating an apple. The last one was a photograph of her dancing with someone. He was good-looking but obviously older, and not as tall. They were smiling at each other. Mason showed the photograph to Kopt. "Is this someone special she's dancing with, that I should know about?"

Kopt shook his large head. "No, that's just Lars Bergstom, one of the editors of the Swedish newspaper she writes for. It was taken last December at the Swedish embassy's Yule Ball in Paris."

"The way they were looking at each other, I thought maybe they had something going."

Kop again shook his head. "No. He may be interested in her, of course, but the reason she is smiling is simply that she loves to dance. Are you a good dancer, Mr. Mason?"

"Not really; but I get by." Mason took the photograph back and looked at it again. Lisa, holding Bergstom's outstretched hand, was making a wide, graceful turn that swept her long blond hair away from her bare shoulders and flared out the bottom of her evening dress. Mason looked at her legs. They were long and shapely, enhanced by high heel dancing slippers. He put the photograph with the others. "You said she writes for a Swedish newspaper?"

"Yes, a daily called 'Idag.' She is freelance and travels around Europe doing articles on whatever she wants."

"Where does she live in Paris?"

"At present, we do not know. Until recently, she was renting a small flat on the Rue St. Geimain. But she has moved, and we do not know where. Since she became suspicious she is being watched, she has not remained very long at any one address." Kopt paused. "However, finding her should not be too difficult in view of her frequency at the Au Pied de

Couchon." He saw Mason was looking at the last photograph again. "Do not be deceived by Fraulein Helms's good looks; she is as intelligent as she is beautiful. She is a graduate of the University of Stockholm, and teaches journalism at the Sorbonne. She is fluent in French, English and Spanish, and of course German."

Mason held up the photograph again. "The guy in here; you said he was nothing special to her. Is there—?"

"—Someone else? No. She was married once, to another writer, but it did not work out. They were divorced and he has gone out of her life. She sees different men from time to time, but is not seriously involved with any of them." Kopt folded his hands, and leaned back on the sofa. "Well, I think I have told you all I need to at this point. Do you have any other questions?"

Mason put the photographs back into the folder, and slipped it into his briefcase. "No, I think I've got the picture."

Kopt smiled. "So, you will take on this matter for us?"

Mason shrugged. "I don't see any reason not to." He stood up. "It's certainly something different, but I'm willing to give it a shot."

Kopt, obviously pleased, hoisted himself up from the sofa, reached out and pumped Mason's hand. "Splendid! Splendid!" He walked Mason to the door. "I am returning to Israel tomorrow. All you need to know is in the folder I gave you. But if you have any questions, remember, you can always reach me through Sawyer at the Chase Manhattan." He stood watching while Mason put on his coat and struggled with his rubbers. He smiled. "Winter is certainly an inconvenience, isn't it?"

Mason, still struggling with one of his rubbers, looked at him. "It's a pain in the ass."

After Mason had left, Kopt waited by the door for a few moments. Then, satisfied Mason was gone, he limped back into the middle of the room. "All right, Seig, you can come out."

From the darkness of the bedroom appeared a huge, giant of a man, well over six feet, with a huge barrel chest, his fierce bearded face scowling at the bright light of the sitting room. Kopt turned to him. "Well, Sieg, did you get a good look at him?"

"*Ja,* I will know him when I see him again."

"The next time will be in Paris. It is likely he will stay at a hotel called the Pont Royal. He may become aware you are following him; I do not care about that. What is important is that he not know why. He must not even suspect that you have any connection with me."

Sieg nodded. "*Ja,* I understand. As always, what you want done will be done."

* * *

"*REI*"

Mason placed his hands on the black belt of his pajama-like *judo-gi* and turned toward the painting of Dr. Jigaro Kano in the corner of the dojo. Together with the others standing with him, he bowed slowly. At the Kodokan, as in every judo school in the world, sessions always began with a tribute to the venerable nineteenth century Japanese physician who first taught occidental man the art of throwing someone twice his weight. Everyone straightened up and turned again to the front of the dojo where Kobe Matsura, sixth degree black belt and founder of the Kodokan, was standing.

"*REI*"

They all bowed to Matsura. Matsura, expressionless, bowed back. Matsura was a Nisei. In 1942, he had seen his family taken from its home in California and interned in a relocation camp in Utah. He had avoided the internment by joining the army's all Nisei 442nd Cornbt Team. The 442nd, sent to fight in the Italian campaign, became the most decorated unit in the war. Matsura, himself, was twice cited for bravery. Despite what the United States had done to his family, Matsura was proud to be an American. He was also proud to be Japanese. Judo, in a sense, epitomized how he felt about both. Derived from the centuries old martial arts of the Orient, it was now a popular American sport, yet remained traditionally Japanese, a unique blend of the two cultures. To Matsura it was important the blend be preserved; he insisted his students, all Americans, learn their judo teems in Japanese. He viewed any technique, however well executed, as less than perfect if not described in the language of Dr. Kano. Mason liked Matsura and respected him. Matsura began speaking.

"Good evening, gentlemen. Tonight is a very special one for all of us. Assistant *Sensei,* Mason-san, is leaving us for a while to go to Europe on business." He looked at Mason. "You are going to Paris?"

"Yes, *Sensei,* to Paris."

Matura bowed slightly toward Mason. "There are worse places your business could take you, is that not so?"

Mason smiled. "Yes, there are worse places."

Matsura motioned to one of the black belts behind Mason. The black belt got up, bowed, and left the dojo. Matsura continued speaking. "Masonsan will be away from us for some time. We will miss him here at the dojo." He paused. "I am going to tell you a story about Mason-san that I have never told before. When he first came to Kodokan, he was already *Sandan;* he had earned his third degree black belt in another dojo while he was in the service. In our dojo at the time were two other ***Sandans.*** Very good Sandans they were too; they had earned their black belts here in Kodokan and had won many trophies in ***shiais*** with other dojos. I told Mason-san I wanted him to ***shiai*** with each of my Sandans. I told him I did not expect him to throw them but, since he was ***Sandan*** and they were ***Sandan,*** he should not be thrown by them either." Matsura paused. I arranged the ***shiai*** between Mason and my ***Sandans.*** When Mason came into the dojo, I was surprised to see he was not wearing his black belt; he was wearing a brown one. He said to me" ***Sensei,*** if I am going to wear a black belt in your dojo, I am going to earn it in your dojo.'" Matsura looked down at Mason. "Remember that, Mason-san?"

Mason nodded.

Matsura, although expressionless, was obviously enjoying himself. "My two ***Sandans*** were never thrown so fast; two of the best ***uchi matas I*** have ever seen!" He looked at Mason. "That's right, isn't it? I've told it right, haven't I?"

Mason smiled. "Well, they really put up more of a fight than you're giving them credit for."

The black belt who had left the dojo returned. He walked to the front of the dojo and handed Matsura a small bronze plaque. Matsura motioned for Mason to come up and stand beside him. "Mason-san, you have been a credit to Kodokan. There is not *a judoka* here who has not benefited from your patient teaching. It is one thing to be a good competitor and throw all one's opponents; and you have many trophies to show that you are strong *judoka* in *shiaL* But there is more to judo than that. It is part of judo to help others of lower rank develop their techniques. That is what the great Dr. Kano has taught us. He would be proud of what you have done here at Kodokan. So, we want you to have this." He held up the plaque and read the inscription on it. "To Mason-san, from his friends at Kodokan."

Mason took the plaque. "Thanks, *Sensei.*" He turned to the class. "And thanks to all of you; I'm going to miss being here." He bowed to Matsura and went back down to stand with the others.

Matsura motioned to one of the other black belts to come up beside him. "I have decided to make Dayton-san new Assistant *Sensei.* He has worked hard to become *Nidan;* he has one of the best *shiai* records in New England." Matsura turned to Dayton. "I don't think you've been beaten this year, have you?"

Dayton responded with a thin smile *"Sensei, I* haven't been beaten by anyone since I became a black belt."

Ed Dayton was twenty-six. In judo less than two years, he had progressed rapidly from white belt to brown belt to black belt, and now to second degree black belt. No one else in the whole New England conference had risen up through the belt ranks as quickly. Five foot seven; he weighed a hundred and ninety pounds, all solid muscle. Obsessed with physical fitness, he spent and hour before every session working out in the weight room. His record in competition with other dojos was phenomenal; he had won more trophies than anyone in the history of the Kodokan. Lacking a smoothness of technique, he had sent many a surprised opponent crashing to the mat with his sheer physical strength. Mason reached up and shook his hand. "Congratulations, Ed, I think you'll make a good Assistant *Sensei.*"

Matsura was speaking again. "Because this is Mason-san's last night with us, we are going to honor him in the traditional way, with a line-up from *Gokyu* white belt to *Aldan* black belt." He paused. "But first, it is time for *randori.*"

Everyone paired off to warm up. Matsura clapped his hands, and the whole dojo was suddenly alive with men in their white *judo-gis* grunting and screaming, flying over one another's shoulders like Raggedy-Andy dolls, and slamming down violently on the thin mat. Dayton picked as his *randori* partner Chuck Inglalls, a big likeable brown belt who had just missed making black belt at the last promotional. Mason was about to pick a partner when Matsura tapped him on the shoulder. "Before you **randori,** I would like to speak to you for a moment outside the dojo."

"Sure, ***Sensei.***"

When they were outside the dojo, Matsura turned to Mason. "Steve, I'm going to miss you. You've really been a good assistant."

"Thanks, Kobe, I'm going to miss this place. I've worked with a lot of different *senseis* in the service; you're the best I've seen."

Matsura almost smiled; instead he bowed. "Ah, like Japanese, you trade compliment for compliment."

"Well, anyway, you're getting a good assistant in Ed Dayton." Matsura frowned. "I'm concerned about Dayton."

"Why? I know he's a little rough on the new students but he works hard and knows his judo. And you have to admit he's a strong competitor."

Matsura nodded. "Yes, there is no question about that. But he still does not seem to understand that there is more to judo than being a strong competitor, that one has to be a patient teacher as well."

"Oh, he may be weak in his teaching, but I think he'll—"

Matsura interrupted him. "Steve, it is in his mind that he can beat you, that you are too much a teacher and not enough a competitor. He has decided he is going to throw you tonight, in front of the whole class."

Mason laughed. "He may do just that. He's a lot younger than I am, and he'll be at the end of the line-up, when I'm the most tired."

Matsura put his hand on Mason's shoulder. "I don't want Dayton to throw you, Steve. I want you to throw him. It will be good for the dojo that you throw him. That is what I want."

Mason looked at Matsura. "I understand, Kobe."

They went back into the dojo and watched Dayton *randori* with the brown belt, Ingalls. Dayton and Inglalls had clasped their hands tightly on each other's *gis* and were shuffling back and forth on the mat, each looking for an opportunity to off balance the other and move in for a throw. Ingalls made several attempts to spin in on Dayton and lift him off his feet. Each time, the new Assistant *Sensei* became a stonewall, and knocked Ingalls to his knees. Matsura turned to Mason. "Yes, Dayton-san is very strong." He paused. "But tonight, Mason-san, you are going to throw him for an *Ippon.*"

Dayton and Inglalls continured to *randori.* Ingalls tried another throw and was knocked to his knees again. As he was getting up, Dayton spun in on him, driving his shoulder up into Ingail's chest. He lifted Ingalls off his feet, turned him upside down, and slammed him on the mat. He looked down at him and smiled. "That's enough *randori* for me; I want to save something for later."

Mason selected one of the brown belts, and warmed up with him until Matsura clapped his hands, signaling the end of the *randorL* Then he waited in the center of the dojo while everyone else withdrew to the side and sat down cross-legged against the wall. Matsura announced the line-up: As usual, the line-up will be in order of belt rank. We will begin with two white belts: Barton-san, *Gokyu,* and Donaldson-san, *Yonkyu:...*

Barton and Donaldson were new students; neither had been studying judo more than six months. Barton was strong and quick but had not yet developed any real technique. Donaldson, still in high school, was showing a flair for the sport. He had done well at the last *shiai* and was close to promotion to brown belt. They both stood up and faced Mason.

"...then three brown belts, Oliver-san, *Sankyu;* Evans-san, *Nikyu;* and Krovitz-san, *Ikkyu;...*"

Oliver, Evans and Krovitz stood up beside Barton and Donaldson. Oliver has just earned his brown belt at the last promotional; it was still new and stiff, and he kept tying and untying it as he waited with the others. Evans and Krovitz were both experienced brown belts.

CC...and fmally, two black belts: Hoak-san, *Shodan;* and Dayton-san, *Nidan.*" Hoak and Dayton stood up to complete the line up.

To the occidental mind, a judo line-up seems inherently unfair: a contest in which one man must fight several, one after the other, each one sapping his strength, weakening him for the next, and each successive opponent higher in belt rank and more dangerous than the last. But in judo, strength, like size, is irrelevant. Only belt rank matters. For a black belt to defeat an opponent of lower rank in a single contest is meaningless; the defeat is inevitable. It is only when the elements of fatigue and stamina are added and he must withstand the relentless assaults of one fresh and increasingly skillful opponent after another, that he can truly demonstrate the skill his belt rank signifies.

Mason looked over the line-up of men he had to fight. The white belts and brown belts would be no problem, although he had to be careful with the *Ikkyu,* Krovitz. It was the black belts, Hoak and Dayton that would be tough. Out of the corner of his eye, he saw that Dayton was smiling. He made a decision; he would save his *unchi mata* until his fight with the new Assistant *Sensei.*

Matsura clapped his hands. *"Reif"*

The seven men facing Mason bowed in unison. Mason bowed back. Then everyone except Barton sat down. Matsura gave the signal to begin. *"Hajime!"*

Mason and Barton grasped each other's *gis* and began shuffling around on the mat. Barton made a primitive attempt at *0 Soto Gari,* the classic leg sweep all beginners in judo must master. Mason easily avoided it. Barton tried it again, without success. He shook his head in frustration. "Goddam it, Steve, I thought I was an athlete, andsI can't seem to get out of my own way."

Mason encouraged him. "Hang in there, Ron, don't give up. We were all beginners once. Keep trying; it'll come to you." He let Barton try a few more times, then pulled the white belt off balance and swept his feet out from under him, dumping him on the mat. Matsura raised his hand. *"Ippon!"* By *De Ashi Harai,* foot sweeping technique." Barton got up. He bowed, then went back and sat down again. Donaldson, the young Yonkyu, who was close to being promoted to brown belt, replaced Barton. Donaldson's judo was better than Barton's but still undeveloped. Mason saw he has nervous, and tried to calm him down. "Well, Bill, I expect to see you wearing a brown belt when I get back from Paris."

Donaldson responded with a youthful smile. "I sure hope so, Mr. Mason."

Mason treated him the same as Barton, letting him try a few throws before spilling him on the mat with a hip technique.

"Ippon/ By *Harai Goshi'*

Oliver, still fmgering his new brown belt, was next. Mason congratulated him on his promotion, then dropped him quickly with a *Tai Otoshi* to deflate his ego a little.

Evans, the next brown belt, was a big strong redhead who liked to take his opponents to the mat where he could use his size and strength to win by a hold-down or choking technique. He did not throw as well as a second-degree brown belt should; but on the mat he was a tough customer. He made it clear right away he wanted to go there, several times letting himself go off balance with Mason so they would fall to the mat together. Mason saw some beautiful openings for a throw but decided to beat Evans at his own game. He let himself be taken to the mat, slipping his fmgers inside the lapels of Evans's *gi* as they fell. Before Evans could work his body into position for a hold-down, it was too late; Mason's fmgers were already tightening the lapels of the big redhead's *gi* around his throat like a garrote. Evans struggled to break the choke but Mason just squeezed tighter. Evans, his face reddening as he struggled to breathe, slapped the mat to signal surrender.

Matsura clapped his hands. ***Ippon!*** By ***Shimewaza!"***

The last brown belt, Sherm Krovitz, was Mason's favorite student. Like Mason, he was tall, with long legs, and had a good ***uchi mata.*** As he took hold of Mason's ***gi,*** he wished him good luck. "Good luck over there in Paris, Steve."

"Thanks, Sherm. Keep working on the old ***uchi maul;*** it's a hell of a throw for guys built like us." The words were hardly out of his mouth before Krovitz was in on him with a try at the inner thigh throw. Krovitz's entry was good, and his leg swept back high like it should. It would have been a perfect throw if he had not forgotten his ***kusushi,*** the all-important off balancing, essential to any throw. Mason reacted reflexively. He grabbed Krovitz's extended leg, arched his back, and swept the brown belt's other leg from under him. Krovitz dropped like a rock to the mat.

"Ippon by—" Matsura hesitated. He looked at Mason. "That was good technique, Mason-san, but I do not know what to call it." He thought for a moment, then raised his arm. ***"Ippon!*** By…by good technique." Everyone laughed. Matsura clapped his hands. "One minute rest."

Mason knelt down on the mat. His *gi* was all outside his belt, and he tucked it in again. He took several deep breaths. The line-up had taken its toll; he was tired. And he still had to contend with the two black belts, Hoak and Dayton. He had to be careful; either one could throw him if he got careless. The minute was almost up. He looked across the mat, and saw that the thin smile was still on Dayton's face.

Matsura gave the signal to continue. *"Yoshi!"*

The first black belt, Hoak, was a *strong judoka.* He had made *Shodan* by steadily progressing up the belt ranks, mastering all the difficult throwing techniques required. No single throw was his favorite; he was good at all of them. You didn't know what to expect. He might spill you on the mat with a subtle foot sweep, or suddenly drop low and send you flying though the air with a spectacular shoulder throw. At the last *shiai,* he beat four straight opponents with four different techniques, the last a picture perfect *Hani Goshi,* one of judo's most difficult hip throws.

As soon as they grasped *gis,* Mason knew he was fighting a black belt. Hoak was not making any mistakes; he was being cautious, not giving Mason any good openings. Mason saw an opening for his *uchi mats* but passed it up. Suddenly, Hoak was in on him, trying for a *seoi nage,* the major shoulder throw that in seconds would have Mason flying over this back. Hoak's *kusushi* was good and, unless Mason did something quickly, he was going to be slammed to the mat for an *ippon.* With every once of strength he had, he twisted his body as he went upside down over Hoak's shoulder. He came down hard on the mat, but landed on his side and not his back.

Matsura shook his head. *"Mosh Gosh!"*The throw was an "almost," not quite good enough to score a point.

The moment Mason was on his feet, Hoak spun in on him again. The two men went off balance and fell together to the mat. Hoak's hands slipped inside Mason's lapels, trying for a choke. Mason broke Hoak's grip, and tried for a hold-down. Hoak twisted out from under him and rolled away.

Matsura clapped his hands. "Fix *gis.*"

Mason and Hoak knelt down on the mat facing each other, and tucked in their *gis.* Mason was glad to have a breather. He was really tired now. He could see Hoak's face was flushed and red. He was sure his own looked worse. Out of the corner of his eye he saw Dayton smiling.

Matsura signaled for them to continue. *"Yoshi!"*

They both got up slowly. Hoak was tired too. He tried another hip throw. Mason was ready this time and countered with a foot sweep that caught Hoak just right and spilled him on the mat.

Matsura's arm shot out to the side. *"Wazari!"*

Hoak got up. "I thought you had me that time, Steve." The *wazari,* half an *ippon,* was enough to give Mason the match if no one scored again.

Hoak, now behind, tried several quick throws that Mason was able to avoid. Matsura raised his hand. "Time."

They stopped fighting, stepped back and bowed to each other. Mason gave Hoak a friendly nudge on the shoulder. "You're tough, George; you almost had me several times."

Matsura lowered his raised arm towards Mason. "Decision, by *wazari.*"

Now, the only one left was Dayton. The new Assistant *Sensei* stood up. He was still smiling. It was clear he could not wait to fight. As soon as he heard *hajime,* he grabbed Mason's lapel and began pushing and pulling him around the mat, trying to off-balance him He spun in on Mason, trying for a hip throw but Mason slipped away from it. Dayton tried again. This time he tripped over Mason's foot and fell down. It was not even a *mosh gosh,* but it gave Mason a breather. The moment Dayton was up, Mason hit him with a combination leg and hip throw that slammed the new Assistant *Sensei* down on the mat.

Matsura's arm shot out to the side. *"'"Wazari*

Dayton scowled at Matsura, objecting to the call. Matsura, expressionless, motioned for him to continue. *"Yoshi!"*

Dayton, still angry, rushed at Mason, grabbing one of his legs and lifting it off the mat. Mason, now on one foot, was vulnerable. He had to keep hopping from side to side to avoid a foot sweep. Dayton tried the foot sweep and missed. He tried a second time, and missed again. Frustrated, he flung Mason to the mat. He waited for Mason to start to get up, then spun in on him for a *seoi nage*. This time he was low enough and his shoulder came up hard into Mason's chest, lifting Mason off his feet and turning him upside down in the air. Mason twisted his body to avoid an *ippon* and landed on his side. Dayton looked at Matsura for the call.

"Wazari!"

The match was now even. Dayton attacked with an *o soto gari* that knocked Mason to his knees. Before he could get up, Dayton was on top of him, trying for a hold-down. Mason, too tired now to grapple with Dayton on the mat, rolled his body into a ball to avoid being pinned and keep the lapels of his *gi* out of Dayton's reach. Dayton struggled for several minutes trying to get a hold-down or choke; then he abandoned the effort and stood up. As Mason was getting up, Dayton spun in on him again. This time, Mason was ready and rolled away. Dayton fell awkwardly on the mat.

Matsura clapped his hands. "One minute rest; fix your *gis.*"

As they knelt down to tuck in their *gis,* Dayton leaned toward Mason. "You look all pooped out, Steve."

"I've got a little left, Ed."

"Yoshi!"

Mason and Dayton got up and went at it again. Mason tried a hip throw but Daytona avoided it. Dayton grabbed the collar of Mason's *gi,* and began twisting it into a choke. Mason leaned back so that Dayton's arm was extended, then spun in and locked the Assistant *Sensei's* arm in a *kanseisuwaza,* the deadly arm bar that will break an opponent's elbow if he does not submit. Dayton winced and let go of Mason's gi. For a moment, the two of them stood apart, catching their breath. Mason could feel he was almost out of gas. He had a *wazari,* but so did Dayton. If neither of them scored again, Matsura would have to declare the match a draw. Dayton might be willing to settle for that, he thought; after all, Dayton was the lower belt rank and could always crow about Mason's not being able to beat him. Dayton's ego wouldn't settle for that, he decided; no, nothing short of throwing Mason for an *ippon* in front of the whole dojo would satisfy him. Mason decided to take a chance. He deliberately left himself open for a *hane goshi,* gambling that Dayton could not execute the difficult hip technique well enough to throw him. Dayton saw the opening, but hesitated. Like Mason, he knew the throw was a difficult one to execute. He decided to combine it with a flying arm bar. Then, if his *hane goshi* didn't work, he'd take Mason to the mat and finish him off with the *kansetsuwaza.* He made his move. His entry was good and as he spun in he locked Mason's elbow tightly in the arm bar. But in concentrating on the two techniques at once, he had forgotten a third the always-essential *kusushi.* Too anxious to execute his deadly combination, he left himself vulnerable with first off-balancing his opponent. It was a fatal error. Mason's balance was still intact when Dayton extended his leg for the *hane goshi.* It was the opening Mason was waiting for. With all the strength had left, he spun in quickly, dropped low, and swept his leg back in an arabesque. His leg caught Dayton on the inner thigh in a perfect *uchi mata.* The new Assistant *Sensei* flew up in the air, flipped over like a playing card., and crashed down on the mat on his back.

Matsura's arm shot up. *"Ippon!* By *uchi mata!"*

Mason, now completely exhausted, managed a quick glance at Matsura. Matsura's face was still expressionless.

—but his eyes were smiling

* * *

The announcement over the plane's intercom had a metallic quality to it. ***"Mesdames et monsieurs, nous allons atterir dans quelques minutes a l'aeroport Charles DeGaulle."*** There was a pause, then: "Ladies and gentlemen, we have begun our descent and will be landing shortly at DeGaulle Airport." It woke Mason. He sat up in his seat, rubbed the sleep out of his eyes, and glanced out the window. It was bright daylight but the plane was still too high to see anything but a blanket of clouds below. He looked at his watch. It was still on Boston time. He spun the hands forward six hours to Paris time.

"Coffee, ***Monsieur?'*** Mason looked up at the pretty Air France stewardess standing by his seat smiling at him. He shook his head; the two Heinekens he had before falling asleep were already pressing on his bladder; coffee would only make things worse. He turned and glanced out the window again. The plane had now descended into the blanket of clouds. He sat back, took out the small French phrase book he had bought at the airport in Boston, and thumbed through it. Reading the French phrases reminded him of Marilyn. He smiled. He had not thought about Marilyn for ages, not since that Christmas a few years ago when he received a card from her and saw that she got married again, for the third time.

Marilyn Andrews, that was her maiden name. He first met her when they were both seniors in college. She came from a well to do family in Connecticut and was a language major. She liked to tease him, teaching him little French phrases, then laughing at the way he pronounced them. They fell in love, convinced they couldn't live without each other. They slept together the last semester and got married right after graduation. Then he had to go into the service, and she went back to live with her parents. When he was in basic training at Fort Dix, he drove up to Connecticut every weekend to see her. When he was shipped overseas, he thought she would go with him. But she said she wanted to stay in Connecticut where she had a good job teaching and could be with her family. So, he went overseas without her. She wrote him a lot at first, even flew out to Hawaii once when he had his first leave. But after that, things changed; her letters became less frequent and different somehow. Finally she wrote him to say there was someone else, someone she thought she had more in common with. Mason thought about asking for special leave to go back and beat the shit out of the guy. But then he decided instead to agree to a divorce and let the guy have her if he wanted her.

After Marilyn, the only other woman he came close to marrying was Denise, the American Airlines stewardess he lived with for a year in

Cambridge. Denise had been around. She was good looking, liked sex, and while not the brightest person he ever knew, was a lot of fun, and he really liked her. When American told her she was being transferred to Dallas, she wanted to quit, and she and Mason talked about getting married. But in the end, she took the transfer and he never saw her again.

Now it was Joanne. He smiled to himself. It was only six months ago she moved into the apartment next to his. In that short time, she had made him read three of her unpublished novels, all of which he liked, redecorated his apartment twice, given him seven collages, painted his portrait, and slept with him, a lot of times without sex. She had turned out to be what no other woman had ever been: a good friend. He remembered the night before his meeting with Kopt, when he told her he was going to Europe. She wanted to know why he was going. When he said he couldn't tell her, she just smiled, said she understood, and would settle for his promise to write. He promised.

The plane continued its descent. The Heinekens were winning the battle with his bladder. He looked at the signs over the two lavatories. Both were occupied.

The metallic voice came over the intercom again. *"Attachez votre ceinture s'il vous plait* . Please fasten your seat belts." Mason glanced again at the signs of over the lavatories. Both still occupied. It was too late now; he would have to wait until he got inside the terminal. He thumbed through the French phrase book to where he had underlined how to ask where the men's room was: ***Ou est les monsieurs?***

* * *

The line to get through Passport Control was long and moving at a snail's pace; and he was still a dozen people back. He knew now he had waited too long; his bladder was about to explode and he was bouncing up and down on one foot. He looked around for a men's room sign but did not see one. He spotted a guy coming out of an unmarked door, still adjusting his pants. Mason left the line, hurried over to the guy, and pointed to the door. *"Monsieurs?"*

The guy shook his head. "Sorry, Mac, I don't speak French; I'm an American."

Mason laughed. "So am I! Is there a toilet in there? My back teeth are floating."

The guy laughed back. "I had the same problem. Yeah, there's one in there. It's for the employees but you can take a leak in there."

"Thanks" Mason hurried past him and went through the door. Inside was a urinal and one stall. He dropped his carry-on bag on the floor, stood up to the urinal and started sending a stream into it. He was still going when the door opened behind him and a woman in an employee's uniform came in. She ignored him and walked past into the stall. Mason, still not finished, shook his head. "Well, I guess this is France all right!"

* * *

. Mason cleared customs and carried his bags out into the terminal where there was a sea of faces scanning the incoming passengers for people they had come to meet. Above one of them, he spotted a hand-lettered sign with the words "WHIT, BROWN, THORN & EMT." Holding it was a neatly dressed young man with a black, Charlie Chaplin moustache. Mason pushed his way through the crowd to where the young man was standing, dropped his bags, and stuck out his hand. "Hi, I'm Steve Mason from Boston."

The young man broke into a smile He put down the sign and pumped Mason's hand. "How do you do, Mr. Mason. I'm Bob Corbit from the Paris Office; I have my car outside." He picked up one of Mason's bags and led the way out of the terminal to the parking lot. He stopped at a small Volkswagen, opened the trunk and stuffed the bag he was carrying into it.

The other one will have to go in the back seat." He apologized for the size of his car. "I should have brought one of the firm's cars. This one's my own. I'm afraid it's going to be a little cramped for you."

" No problem; I'll manage." They got in and drove out of the parking lot on to a three lane highway. "I appreciate your coming to the airport to meet me, Bob."

"Mr. Deschamps wanted to be sure someone met you. I volunteered because I live out this way and it's easy for me to swing by the airport on my way to the office. Have you been to Paris before?"

"No, this is my first time."

"You'll love it; it's a great city."

"How long have you been over here. Bob?"

"Almost three years now. I'll be finished with my Paris Office tour of duty in a couple of months, then it's back to Boston. I've liked it here but I'll be glad to get back home. I'm anxious to see that new Quincy Market area; I hear it's really something.

Mason nodded. "It's nice; it's a fun place to go."

Corbit ran his forger along the bottom of his moustache. "Sounds like a pretty heavy matter you've come over here on, Mr. Mason."

"Oh? What have you heard about it?"

"Not much, really, just that its potentially a big lawsuit for some new important client, and the company on the other side is Chimique Industrielle."

"You've heard of them?"

"Oh sure, they're a big chemical company here in Europe." "What about our client, Hoch?"

Corbit shook his head. "I'd never heard of them until I saw their name on the new clients list. I guess they're a big Gelman company, though. One of their engineers is already in our office working on the case."

"What's he like?"

"He has the office next to mine so I see him all the time. He's working hard on the case, I know that." Corbit smiled. "But he's also sort of a fun guy."

"What do you mean?"

Corbit's finger was at this moustache again. "Well, I've had lunch with him a few times. He loves French food and is always trying out new restaurants he's heard about. And he likes to sit on the Champs Elysees and watch the girls walk by. He told me the other day he thought Paris had the best looking women in the world."

"Is he French?"

"No, German, or Austrian, I think. His name is Carl, Carl Dietz. But he studied chemical engineering at Cal Tech and talks like an American. He broke his arm skiing in Grenoble just before he came to work in the office. It's all in a cast; he bumped into a tree or something But it doesn't seem to slow him down at all; he's working like hell on the case."

Mason stretched his long legs out as far as they would go under the Volkswagen's dashboard. "What about Deschamps? I've never met him. What kind of a guy is he?"

Corbit shrugged. "He's okay, maybe a little carried away with being the head of the Paris Office. He spends most of his time dealing with the French lawyers we have to use over here. Most of the work is done by French lawyers; our job is just liaison. He has a French name and speaks the language like a native, but he's an American like you and me. His family are all Boston bluebloods from Beacon Hill. All in all, though, he's not a bad guy to work for." Corbit paused. "The guy you really want to get to know is our office manager, Andre Doucette."

"I assume he's French."

Corbit laughed. "As the Eiffel Tower. If there's anything at all you want to know about Paris, he's the one to ask." They were coming into Paris now. The highway had become an elevated four lane expressway, below which Mason could see the streets of the city on both sides. He took his itinerary out of his pocket and looked at it. "They've got me staying at the Pont Royal. What kind of place is that, do you know?"

"It's okay. It's over on the Left Bank and it's very French. Doucette must have picked it. He takes care of making the hotel arrangements for the office and always picks a very French one unless he's told otherwise. But the Pont Royal is okay. And it has a neat little bar."

Corbit took one of the downramps off the expressway into the middle of the hectic Paris traffic that seemed to be going every which way at once. Even on the sidewalks, everyone seemed to be hurrying somewhere. Corbit took a short-cut through a maze of narrow back streets that brought them to a small open square where Mason could see the Seine in the distance. Corbit pulled over to the curb and stopped. "Well, here we are."

The Pont Royal was inauspicious. Except for a small sign over the entrance, it looked like the apartment buildings all around it. A uniformed doorman came out, took Mason's bags, and led them inside. Mason stepped up to the desk and began filling out the registration foul'. He turned to Corbit. "Deschamps isn't expecting to see me at the office today, I hope."

Corbit shook his head. "No, he doesn't expect you until tomorrow. He knew you would be tired and want time to get settled. He's planning to meet with you first thing tomorrow morning." Corbit waited for Mason to finish the registration form, then added. "If you want me to, I can recommend a restaurant you might want to try tonight."

"I was given the names of a few places before I left; but I'm open to suggestions. What's the name of the place?"

"The Cloche D'Or. It's on the Left Bank, a taxi ride but not too far from here."

The desk clerk tapped a little bell and gave Mason's key to a waiting bellman. The ***chausser*** will show you to your room, ***monsieur. I*** hope you have a pleasant stay with us."

The bellman led Mason and Corbit across the lobby and into a small cage elevator. Corbit finished telling Mason about the Cloche D'Or. "It's sort of a fusty place but it's fun to eat there. And the food is out of this world."

Mason nodded. "Sounds good. Maybegive it a try."

Mason's room was on the top floor. It had a comfortable sitting area and its windows were a pair of French doors overlooking the street in front of the hotel and, in the distance, the Seine. Corbit tipped the bellman, then turned to Mason. "This is the best room in the place. It's the one the office uses for big clients and important French lawyers from out of town." He paused and smiled. "And for important partners from the Boston Office."

Mason laughed. He went over to the French doors, pulled the curtain aside and looked out. "So, that's the Seine, off there in the distance?"

"That's right. Sometimes you can see the boats going up and down. That big building on the left is the Louve. And way off to the right, where you see the two spires, that's Notre Dame."

"It's quite a view."

Corbit walked over to the French doors. "There's another view from here that's interesting. It's not something I point out to clients, although I'm sure a lot of them notice it anyway." He pointed to the building across the street. "See that window to the left of the fire escape, not the one on the top floor, the one just under it."

"Yeah, what about it?"

"The apartments in that building are all expensive as hell. That one belongs to a call girl with a special clientele. Sometimes, when she's got a customer, she doesn't bother to pull down the shades, and you can see right into the bedroom from here. One of the lawyers we work with from Lyons was telling me about watching her one night. He didn't go into detail but I guess it was a pretty wild scene." Corbit turned away from the French doors. "Well, I've got to run along."

Mason walked him to the door. "Thanks again, Bob, for the lift in from the airport." They shook hands, and Corbit left.

Mason could feel his jet lag. He decided to unpack later. He telephoned down to the concierge and asked for a wake up call at six; then he kicked off his shoes, unloosened his tie, and flopped on the bed. His head had hardly hit the pillow before he was asleep.

Mason was snuggled in bed with Joanne, holding her in his arms in the dark. They had made love and were lying naked, their arms and legs still wrapped around each other. The doorbell of her apartment was ringing. It was a persistent, annoying ring. Joanne had fallen asleep and he was sure it was going to wake her up. The doorbell kept ringing. He did not want to get up and answer it. Who the hell could it be, anyway? What time was it? Wait a minute, he was not in Joanne's apartment; this was not her bed; she wasn't there in his arms. He opened his eyes. The ringing was not a doorbell; it was the telephone beside his bed at the Pont Royal. He reached over and picked it up.

"*Excusez-moi, monsieur.*" You wished to be called at six o'clock."

Mason was fully awake now. He sat up, dangled his feet over the edge of the bed for a few moments, then stood up. Through the French doors he could see that it was now dark outside. He turned on the light in the room and unpacked. He took off all his clothes, shaved, and then treated himself to a long hot shower.

The night air, drifting up the ***Rue de Bac*** from the Seine, had a chill in it. Seig could feel it on the back of his neck as he got out of the car. He turned up the collar of his topcoat and hurried across the street to the corner opposite the hotel. He stepped into the shadows, lit one of his long Turkish cigarettes, and waited.

In all the years he had known Kopt, Seig had never seen him as obsessed as he was with this matter of the German, Molte, and the American, Mason. Seig had known Kopt for a long time, since 1945 when they were both interned in a displaced persons camp in Coblenz. Seig had been brought there from Auschwitz where he had survived an unbelievable three years as a Kapo. Some said he survived because he was only half Jewish and his father, a German, had served in the First World War. The truth was he had survived simply because of his extraordinary size and strength. When the Jews were being shot, strong Kapos were needed to dig the mass graves into which the endless cartloads of corpses had to be dumped. When gas chambers and crematoria replaced the shooting, again it was Seig's strength and stamina that persuaded the Germans to spare his life.

But he was not the only survivor of Auschwitz at Coblenz. One night he awoke to find his hands and feet tightly bound with the bootlaces of others who had witnessed his favored treatment as a Kapo, and were now standing over his bed, planning to take revenge. They would have killed him had not Kopt, who held a position of influence in the camp, intervened. From then on, Seig, like Otto Rothman, felt he owed his life to Kopt and followed him everywhere, from camp to camp, and eventually to Palestine.

In Palestine during the early years, he served as Kopt's personal bodyguard insuring that, although Kopt was an ardent Zionist, he remained immune from Arab harassment. Rare was the Arab who had not heard stories of how Seig dealt with anyone foolish enough to trifle with that immunity. Once, in 1947, two young Arabs fired Sten guns at the windows of Kopt's house. No one was injured, and the damage was minimal. One of the bullets, however, ricocheted off the metal window bolt and struck the post of the bed where Kopt was sleeping. Later that night, the two youths were delivered to a British army hospital where the handles and breeches of their Sten guns had to be hack-sawed off before the barrels could be surgically removed from their rectums. The rumor was that Seig had threatened to pull the triggers. He might as well have. Both the young Arabs bled to death anyway.

Seig dropped the stub of his cigarette on the sidewalk, and crushed it out with the heel of his shoe. He lit another cigarette, and continued to watch the front of the hotel.

* * *

Mason took a clean shirt out of the dresser, and walked over to the French doors. The Louve and the other distant buildings of the city had disappeared into the darkness. All he could see now were tiny lights that seemed far away. He looked down. In front of the hotel, people were scurrying along the sidewalks. Only one figure was stationary: a man standing alone on the corner across the street. His coat was open and Mason could see he had a large barrel chest over which he was wearing a gray vest.

Mason finished buttoning his shirt and slipped on a tie. He glanced across at the call girl's apartment. The bedroom was lighted but empty. He picked up the phone and dialed the concierge. It rang several times, then someone answered.

"*Alto?*"

"This is Mr. Mason in room 612."

"*Oui, monsieur?*"

"I'd like you to make a reservation for me at a restaurant called the Cloche d'Or, for tonight at 7:30."

"Of course. Will it be for just one?"

"Yes, just one."

"I will call you back, *monsieur.*"

As Mason hung up, he glanced out through the French doors again. The man with the gray vest was still there. In the apartment across the street, the call girl had just walked into her bedroom. She was wearing a white satin robe and looked as if she had just taken a bath. Her long black hair hung like a shinny ribbon down her back. She took some clothes from a closet and disappeared from his sight. Mason left the French doors and went back to getting dressed. He had just fmished when the phone rang.

"*Bonsoir, monsieur. I* have made your reservation at the Cloche D'Or for 7:30."

Mason thanked him and hung up. He looked down through the French doors again. On the street, a black limousine had pulled up in front of the call girl's apartment. Mason glanced up at the window and saw that the girl was now dressed. She had piled her hair into an up do and was wearing a long evening gown that was cut low in front to reveal the fullness of her breasts, and slit up the side so her stockinged leg flashed into view each step she took. She slipped on a pair of high-heeled shoes and wrapped a fur piece around her shoulders. After making an entry in a small notebook on the night table, she glanced around the room, then snapped off the light. Mason looked down at the street. A man was standing beside the limousine, holding the door open, waiting. He was middle-aged and was wearing a tuxedo. Mason watched until the call girl came out, got into the limousine, and they drove off together. As the limousine passed the corner across from the hotel, Mason noticed that the man with the gray vest was no longer there. He turned away from the French doors and looked at his watch. It was time to go. He put on his coat, made sure he had the key to the room, and left.

* * *

The Cloche D Or had only eleven tables. Occupying what was once the elegant sitting room of a nineteenth century town house, it was the only restaurant on the otherwise residential *Rue Lezarde.* The tables were arranged so that Henri, who owned the Cloche and waited on it patrons, could display his talents at a small serving table in the center of the room. Henri, fiercely proud of his kitchen, considered to be one of the best in Paris, used his serving table as an actor uses the stage, giving a performance with each course he presented. This combination of the Cloche's haute cuisine and Henri's *petit theatre* provided a unique charm that the patrons of the restaurant insisted could not be matched in all of Paris.

Henri himself greeted Mason at the door. *"Bonsoir, monsieur. Avez-vous reserve?"*

"I'm Mr. Mason."

Henri checked his reservation list, then seated Mason at one of the tables and handed him a menu. *"Desirez-vous an aperitif?"*

Mason, remembering something Joanne had told him, ordered a kir. He looked around the small room. Two tables away, a thin elderly woman was sitting alone sipping her aperitif as she studied the menu. Next to her, three couples stood waiting for Henri to push several of the tables together as one. The only other diner was a small, dwarfish man with a salt and pepper beard who was keeping up a continuous conversation with Henri and was obviously a regular patron of the Cloche.

Henri returned with Mason's kir, and began reciting the evening's courses. *"Ce soir, je vous recommande mon plat du jour. Il est excellent; c'est ."* His French was too fast for Mason to follow. Mason let him finish, nodded, and then looked at the menu. It was entirely in handwritten French, as unintelligible as Henri's recital. Mason could not make any sense at all out of it. He continued to study it, trying to find some phrase or even word that looked familiar.

Henri seated the three young couples, then stopped to talk with the dwarfish man. Their conversation was brief but animated, ending with a joke about something that made them both laugh.

While Mason was absorbed in trying to decipher the menu, another diner entered the room and waited to be seated. He whispered something to Henri who led him to the table next to Mason's. Mason glanced up casually. His eyes widened; it was the man in the gray vest. There was no question about it; Mason would recognize him anywhere. He was even bigger than he appeared from the hotel. He had to weigh two fifty, maybe more, Mason estimated. The man sat down, listened to Henri's recital of the evening's courses, then waved away the menu and ordered. His French, although fluent, was monotonic, obviously not his native tongue. His face reminded Mason of Matsura's: completely expressionless with eyes that shifted back and forth, watching everything. Henri brought him a small bottle of wine, wet the bottom of his glass, and waited for his nod of approval. Then, after filling his glass, came over to Mason's table.

"Etres-vous pret?"

Mason looked again at the menu. He still could not decipher it. It was time for a diversionary action, he decided. He pointed to his kir. "I'll have another one of these." Henri nodded and left.

Mason looked casually around the room. The man with the gray vest was sipping his wine and smoking a long black cigarette. His eyes met Mason's for an instant; then he looked away. Mason frowned. It's no coincidence that the guy picked this restaurant; the bastard's got to be following me for some reason. But why? I've heard about Neo-Nazi organizations that protect guys like Molte; maybe he belongs to one of them and they've somehow found out why I'm over here. Maybe he's working for Kopt. But why the hell would Kopt have someone following me? No, that doesn't make any sense. He's following me, though, that's for sure. Mason glanced at him again. He was now eating his appetizer and seemed completely disinterested in anything else.

Mason's attention was drawn to the center of the room. Henri, now preparing to serve the dwarfish man his main course, was holding a large silver tray on which there were several covered dishes and, in the middle, a tall paper bag tied at the top. He placed the tray on the serving table, paused for a moment to make sure everyone was watching him, then began his performance. Pretending to be oblivious to his audience, he took a large carving knife, stepped back and stood poised like one of the three musketeers, his arm extended, the knife pointing at the serving table. Then, suddenly, he lunged forward and with a rapier-like stroke sliced off the top of the paper bag. The bag exploded in a billow of steam that rose in a single cloud to the ceiling He lunged again and with two perpendicular strokes quartered the bag so its four sides fell outward like the petals of a flower. There, at the bottom of the bag, was a thick juicy steak, still sizzling The dwarfish man broke into a broad smile and clapped his hands with delight. Henri served him. Then taking out his small pad of paper and a pencil, he addressed his attention to Mason again. ***"Que desirez-vous,vous plait?"***

This was it; no more diversionary actions; Henri's pencil was tapping the small pad impatiently; it was time to order. Mason thought for a moment, then pointed to the man in the gray vest. "I'll have whatever he's having, and the same wine too."

Henri nodded and left. Mason smiled to himself If the bastard is going to be following me, I might as well get some use out of him.

* * *

The next morning, when Mason arrived at the Paris Office, his first impression was he had walked into a private home. In a sense, the impression was correct. The space occupied by Whitaker, Brown, Thorndike & Templeton at 23 *Avenue Anatole France* had once been the large duplex apartment of a wealthy Parisienne, convicted of being a collaborator during World War II. Most of the apartment's lavish furnishings were long gone, replaced by the sterile desks, file cabinets and other pedestrian equipment of a law office. A few vestiges of its quaint pre-war character still remained, however, thanks to Deschamps insistence on preserving what he could of its old world French charm.

Mason identified himself to the receptionist and waited in what had been the apartment's foyer, a spacious oval room with curved staircases that swept up the sides like parentheses to the second floor. Above him hung a huge chandelier that seemed to fill the whole ceiling Its long prismatic crystals were catching the morning sunlight, splintering it into thousands of tiny rainbows. He was looking up admiring it when he saw someone coming down one of the staircases. He knew right away it was Deschamps. Tall and fastidiously dressed, he had that unmistakable air of self-confidence and superiority Boston Brahmins seen to inherit at birth. He reached the bottom of the stairs, strode across the foyer, and extended his hand. "Hello, Steve, I'm Lloyd Deschamps. Welcome to Paris. It's nice to have you with us." He turned to the receptionist. "I'm going to show *Monsieur* Mason around a bit; then we'll be in my office."

Deschamps gave Mason a walking tour of the Paris Office.

CC...This was the woman's living room. As you can see, it's now our library..."

...Here, our conference room was her dining room. Under the table I have kept the ornate foot pedal she used to summon her cook . ."

"...That little waiting room with the telephone was once a small pantry..."

"...This area, which we use as a secretarial pool, was a solarium . ."

"...The offices along this hall were all bedrooms"

The tour ended at Deschamps's office, a large corner office richly paneled in polished oak, the floor covered with a thick crimson carpet. In place of a desk was a *Louis Quartorze* writing table, beside it a large globe of the world. Facing the writing desk were two identical wing chairs separated by a small marble coffee table on which the only object was a bronze bust of John F. Kennedy. Deschamps motioned Mason to one of the chairs and closed the door. "This particular room has an interesting history. The German officer with whom the woman was living during the occupation used it as a study. After the war, she was convicted of collaboration and put through all that head shaving business. And of course they confiscated all her property." He shook his head. "I must say, though, I do wish they had left some of her furniture. I've seen pictures of it, and it was really quite irreplaceable."

A question occurred to Mason. "What happened to the German officer she was living with?"

"That's part of the interesting history. He was shot dead right here in this room. Three members of the French underground burst in on him one night when he was sitting there, where my desk is, and just blasted away with Sten guns." Deschamps pointed to one of the bookcases. "You can still see some of the bullet holes there." He settled into the other wing chair. "Well, enough history; let's talk about the present. I understand you're staying at the Pont Royal."

"That's right."

"Is it satisfactory?"

"It's fine."

"The Pont is one of Doucette's favorites. I believe he knows the owner quite well. Of course, if you'd like something a bit more American, I'm sure we can—"

Mason shook his head. "No, it's fine, really."

"Speaking of Doucette, you haven't met him yet, have you?" "No, not yet."

"He's quite a remarkable chap, actually. We're very fortunate to have him. He—"

The door opened. It was Deschamps's secretary. *"Excusezmoi. Voulez-vous du café?"*

Deschamps spoke to her in French. *"Oui,vous plait. Et je voudrais que vous demander a monsieur Doucette de venir dans un instant."* He turned to Mason. "I told her to bring some coffee and ask Doucette to join us."

"Good. I'd like to meet him. You were saying something about being fortunate to have him."

"Yes. The man has an incredible number of contacts in Paris. He seems to have relatives and friends everywhere: the hotels, the restaurants, at the airport, everywhere."

Mason smiled. "That could be useful. There are some things I may need his help with."

"Well, whatever they are, I'm sure he'll be able to be of assistance." Deschamps changed the subject. "I had a telephone conversation yesterday with Alex Templeton. He told me a little about the matter you'll be working on over here. This fellow Kopt sounds like rather an odd chap; but then, you've met him, haven't you?"

Mason nodded. "Yes, I spent several hours with him at his hotel in Boston. Had you ever heard of him before Templeton called you?"

Deschamps shook his head. "No. I'd never heard of his company, Hoch, either. After Alex's call, I took the trouble to look them both up in our directory. They're both in there, of course. Hoch actually is quite a large company. I was surprised, however, to see that despite its German name it's entirely owned by Israelis."

Deschamps's secretary brought in coffee and put it on the marble table between them. ***"Monsieur Doucette sera ici dans un moment."***

Deschamps waited until she had left, then continued. "I'm familiar, of course, with the other company, Chimique. They're a well-known company here in France. The French lawyer who acts for them is a member of my club." Deschamps poured the coffee into two small cups. "From what Alex told me, it appears this fellow Kopt is extraordinarily wealthy and could be a lucrative client for us."

Mason nodded. "Very lucrative."

Deschamps leaned over the coffee table. "Steve, I want you to know I fully understand how important this matter of yours is to the whole firm. If there's anything I can do to help, I want you to be sure to—"

The door opened and into the room stepped a man who was a perfect contrast to Deschamps. Short, barely five feet tall and overweight, he was wearing a suit that could have been bought for someone two sizes smaller. His shirt looked uncomfortably tight, his tie was askew, with the thin end much too long, and several inches of his black socks showed between the cuffs of his trousers and his shoes. Under his sharp beak of a nose was a thin moustache that looked as if it had been drawn with a pencil. Overall, though, his appearance was warm and friendly and the smile on his face seemed genuine. Deschamps stood up. "Ah, Andre! Come and meet ***Monsieur*** Mason from our Boston Office."

Doucette waddled across the room and put out his hand. ***"Monsieur*** Mason, it is a great pleasure to meet you. It is my wish to be of whatever service I can."

Mason shook Doucette's hand. "It's a pleasure to meet you, Andre. Mr. Deschamps tells me you know just about everyone in Paris."

Doucette laughed. "No, no, not everyone. Paris is a large city, ***monsieur.*** It is true I have many friends here, not big people in important positions, you understand, only little people with small jobs." He paused and smiled. "But they are, one might say, situated where, from time to time, they can be helpful."

Deschamps cleared his throat. "Steve, unless there's something else you think we should talk about, I suppose you'd like to go along and get settled in your office." He turned to Doucette. "Why don't you show ***Monsieur*** Mason where his office is, and introduce him to that Hock fellow." He reached over and shook Mason's hand again. "Well, as I said before, welcome to Paris. And remember, if there's anything you think I can do to help yon, just shout out."

Mason nodded. "Okay, thanks." He followed Doucette out of Deschamps's office. As they walked down the hall, Mason decided to test the Office Manager's reservoir of knowledge. "Andre, what do you know about a restaurant called the Pied de Couchon?"

Doucette winced at Mason's French. "It is a very good restaurant, ***monsieur.*** It is in the old ***Les Halles*** section. It is nice and not expensive; I would recommend it."

"I don't suppose you have any contacts there?"

Doucette laughed. "But of course, ***monsieur.*** The ***Maitre D'hotel,*** Francois, is a friend of mine."

"Do you know him well?"

Doucette shrugged. "We were ***Pollus*** together."

"You were in the service together?"

"Yes, during the war. I had occasion to save his life one time. Is there something special I can do for you regarding the Pied?"

"Not right now, Andre, thanks But I may want to ask a favor later."

Doucette nodded. "Of course. If there is anything, just tell me." He stopped outside one of the rooms. "This, *monsieur*, is your office."

They went inside and Mason looked around. The room was small but adequate, with a desk, two chairs and a bookcase full of legal treatises. A single, semi-circular window looked out on the building next door.

Mason started to walk over to the window and bumped his head on the slanted ceiling. Doucette frowned. "I was not told you were so tall, *monsieur*. If this room is not comfortable, I can arrange another."

Mason rubbed his head. "Don't bother, Andre, this will do fine. After I bang my head a few times, I'll learn to duck." He paused.

"By the way, where is this fellow Dietz's office?"

"It is the one right next to this one. Would you like me to go and get him?"

Mason shook his head. "No, let's both go in and you can introduce me.'

* * *

In the office next to Mason's, a man about his age was busily working behind a desk covered with manila folders full of papers. He was blond with deep brown eyes and was wearing thick horn rimmed glasses. A plaster cast covered his left arm up to the elbow. He stood up as Mason and Doucette entered. "Hi, Andre."

"*Bonjour, Monsieur* Dietz. This is *Monsieur* Mason. You have been expecting him." Doucette turned to Mason. "This is *Monsieur* Dietz from the Hoch company."

Mason shook Dietz's hand. 'Hello, Carl, I understand we're going to be working together."

"Hi, Steve, glad you're here. I've got a lot of things to report to you."

Doucette coughed. "*Excusez-moi, monsieurs,* unless there is something else, I will leave you to get acquainted with each other." He paused for a moment, then left.

Dietz motioned to a wooden chair in front of his desk. "Have a seat, Steve."

Mason moved a pile of folders off the chair and sat down. He looked around the Hoch engineer's office. There were manila folders piled everywhere: on his desk, on a table in the corner, on another wooden chair, even on the floor. One wall was covered with aerial photographs of chemical plants and block diagrams Mason recognized as schematics of the Hoch process Chimique was imitating. On the opposite wall was a full size blow up of Marilyn Monroe in a bathing suit. Dietz pointed to his cast. "I got this dumb thing trying to show off at Grenoble just before I came here." He laughed. "Boy, did I feel stupid in the hospital there. Everyone else had broken legs, twisted knees, sprained ankles: the kind of injuries you're supposed to get skiing. And there I was with a broken arm.'" He shook his head. No only was I a lousy skier, I couldn't even get hurt the way you're supposed to." He shrugged. "Well at least it's my left arm, so I can still write and work on the case. Speaking of the case, do you want me to bring you up to date now, or do you want to wait until later?"

Mason opened his briefcase and took out a pad of yellow lined paper. "No, go ahead. This is as good a time as any for me to get an idea of where we are. Don't go into a lot of detail; I'll get that later. Just give me a brief summary."

"Okay. As I go along, if you have any questions, stop me; I'll try to answer them." He waved his hand at the plethora of folders in the room. "You can see I've been doing some work here. I've been at it now for a couple of weeks, and I think I've got a pretty good handle on things." He paused. "Before I give you a report, there's something I want to say first." He looked across the pile of folders on his desk at Mason. "I'm a chemical engineer, Steve; the technology in this case is right up my alley. But you're the one who's in charge; I'm just here to help you. I don't know the first thing about lawsuits. So far as I'm concerned, I think they're a dumb way to try to resolve anything."

Mason smiled. "They are. Sometimes, though, they can't be avoided."

Dietz frowned. "Well, I sure don't understand this one. The process is ours; it's been ours for years. And now this French company comes along and starts using it. I don't see why we can't just show that it's ours and make them stop." He saw Mason smiling, and laughed. "I know, I know, that's why I'm the engineer, and you're the lawyer." He lifted his cast off the desk and rested it in his lap. "Anyway, to me the most important thing I can be doing right now is working on this case. It involves millions of the company's bucks, and the way I see it I couldn't be doing anything more important for my career."

"I'm sure we're going to make a good team, Carl. I've read your resume and I'm glad to have someone with your background on this case. I'd be lost tackling a case like this without someone with your expertise." He paused. "Incidentally, was Kopt the one who assigned you to the case?"

Dietz laughed. "Hell no, I've never even met him. He's the head of the whole company. I don't think even my boss, the chief of the process department, has ever met him. But I know from what my boss told me, that Mr. Kopt considers this thing very important." Dietz looked down at a sheet of paper on which he had made some notes. "I've already done something I thought you'd want me to do before you got here. I've set up a meeting with our Sales Manager in Amsterdam, a guy named Rijksmeer. He's been one of our biggest producers. We've done a lot of business out of his office, and it's the place where we've got the best evidence that Chimique's screwing us. I figured you'd want to get to him first in case it leaks out that the company's shutting down sales offices." He paused. "I don't want you to think I'm trying to run the case."

Mason shook his head. "No, I'm glad you did that. When is the meeting set up?"

Dietz referred to his notes. "The day after tomorrow. I've taken care of the plane and hotel reservations."

Mason nodded. "Okay, what else?"

Dietz handed him one of the folders of papers. "In there you'll find a memo I've put together listing all the other Sales Managers in order of their importance. Under each one, I've written down what we know about him: what the volume of his office has been; what contacts he has had with Chimique; things like that. There's also a proposed schedule in there for meeting with them. I've only set up dates for two others besides Rijksmeer; the rest I figured I'd set up after you've had a chance to look over the schedule." He handed Mason a typewritten list. This is a list of the files I've made up so far. There's so much material, I thought you'd want to have some sort of index."

Mason stuffed the papers Dietz had given him into his briefcase. "Look's like you've been busy, Carl."

"Yeah, I have." Dietz took off his glasses. "But I wouldn't want you to think I haven't found time to enjoy myself here." He smiled. "Paris is really a great city. Is this your first time here?" "Yes, How about you?"

"I was here once before but only briefly; on my way to somewhere else. This is the first time I've had a chance to really see the place. I'm from

Heidelberg, which is nice; but this Paris is something else." He paused. "By the way, where are you staying?"

"The Pont Royal."

Dietz laughed. "Doucette! It had to be Doucette who picked the place. Kind of stuffy, isn't it?"

Mason shrugged. "It's okay. Where are you staying?"

"The Paris Hilton. A lot of the airlines put their stewardesses up there, so the place really swings, which I like. And the restaurant there is not too bad. Speaking of restaurants, what about having dinner together tonight, or do you have other plans?"

"I don't have other plans. Sure, let's do it."

"Great! But let's not do the Hilton; I ate there last night." "Someone gave me the name of a restaurant I'm supposed to try while I'm over here. Maybe you've heard of it."

"What's the name of it?"

"The Pied de Cochon. Ever hear of it?"

"No. But, hey, I'm all for trying something new." Dietz reached in the drawer of his desk and took out a small red book. "Lei's see what my little restaurant guide says about it." He flipped through the pages. "Here it is: ***Au Pied de Cochon, Rue Coquillere 45."*** Sounds good to me. I'll ask Doucette to make us a reservation. How about nine o'clock? I put a call in this afternoon to our Sales Manager in Frankfurt; I left word I'd wait here until seven-thirty for him to call back."

"Nine is fine."

"That's not too late for you?"

"No, it will give me a chance to look over this material you gave me."

"I'll come by your hotel about eight-thirty."

They both stood up. They shook hands and Mason left to go back to his new office.

* * *

Mason tossed his coat on the bed and looked at the two postcards he had bought downstairs in the lobby of the Pont Royal. He decided to send the one with the Eiffel Tower on it to his secretary, the other, showing the artists at Montmartre, to Joanne. He called room service, ordered two Heinekens, then sat down with the postcards. He scribbled a perfunctory greeting on the one to his secretary and wrote a long note on the one to Joanne. When he fmished, he stripped to his shorts, did seventy-five push-ups, and then went into the bathroom to shave and shower.

He had progressed as far as putting on clean underwear and socks when the bellman knocked at the door with the two Heinekens. Mason motioned for him to put them on the dresser, tipped him, and finished getting dressed. He opened one of the beers and walked over to the French doors. It was dark outside and the streets were deserted. Across from the hotel a black Mercedes was parked but he could not see whether anyone was in it. His eyes shifted to the apartment Corbit had pointed out. The bedroom was dark but there was a light on in the living room and he could see the girl walking back and forth. She had on a white blouse unbuttoned at the top and tied in a knot around her bare midriff, and was wearing tan pantaloons tucked into tight calf-length leather boots with spiked heels. Around her waist was a wide leather belt with a heavy gold buckle. A floppy beret was tilted down over one side of her face. Mason watched as she unfolded a small table in the center of the room, covered it with a red cloth, and then disappeared from view. She returned carrying a candle, a bottle of wine and two long stem glasses. She put them on the table and disappeared again. She was gone only a moment and came back with something else she put on the table. Mason could not tell what it was at first. Then he recognized it. It was a small artist's palette complete with paints and brushes.

Down on the street he saw the same limousine from the night before pull up in front of the building. This time the man, dressed in a business suit, went directly into the building without waiting. The limousine drove away.

Mason left the French doors, walked back across the room, and turned on the television set. It came on in the middle of a rerun of "The Hustler" dubbed in French. He opened the second Heineken and sat down on the edge of the bed to watch. Paul Newman, drunk and overconfident, was losing a game of pool to Jackie Gleason. Both of them were jabbering away in French as if it were their native tongue. Mason tried to follow what they were saying but, even though he had seen the movie before, he could not understand them. He got up and went back to the French doors.

The man was now in the girl's apartment, sitting with her at the small table. He was not longer wearing his business suit; he had changed into a short black kimono below which Mason could see his bare hairy legs. He was holding the girl's hand and, with one of the brushes, was carefully painting her fmgernails. He finished one hand and did the other. Then, taking another brush and using a different color, he painted up across the backs of the hands. She turned her hands over so he could paint the palms She was leaning over the candlelight, watching him and smiling, every now and then taking the hand he was not painting to refill his glass or reach under the table to him. She lifted the sleeves of her blouse so he could paint under her arms. She handed him a brush with a delicate tip, then tilted her head back so he could paint long slow strokes down her neck. His brush reached the top of her breasts and she untied her blouse for him. He began painting her bare breasts, tracing smaller and smaller circles, closer and closer to her nipples, now hard and erect and extended towards him

Mason's attention was distracted by a disturbance in the street below. He looked down and saw a police car, its blue light flashing, stopped beside the parked Mercedes. Two *gendarmes* were bending down arguing through the window with the driver. The driver got out. Mason's eyes widened. It was the man in the gray vest. Mason swore under his breath. The bastard's back again tonight! He watched while Gray Vest argued with the *gendarmes* for several minutes, then threw up his arms in exasperation, climbed back into the Mercedes, and drove off. Mason quickly grabbed something on the writing table and scribbled down the license number: DX771P. He looked at what he had written the number on. It was the postcard to Joanne. He glanced again at the girl's apartment. They were both gone from the table. A light was on in the bedroom but the shade was down. Mason glanced back at the living room. The candle had been snuffed but was still on the table, along with the empty wine bottle and the two glasses. On the floor, beside the chair where the girl had been sitting, was her blouse and spiked-heels boots. Mason looked again at the table. The paints and brushes were not there. As he turned from the

French doors, the telephone rang. It was the concierge. ***Bonsoir.*** There is a ***Monsieur*** Dietz here to see you."

"Tell him I'll be right down."

Mason grabbed his coat, turned off Paul Newman in the middle of a pool shot, and left.

* * *

To reach the *Au Pied de Cochon,* its patrons have to climb a steep flight of narrow wooden stairs leading up from the cobble stoned *Rue Coquillere* to the second floor of the old market building in *Les Halles,* where the restaurant has been for more than fifty years. *Les Hanes,* at one time the home of the busy shops of Paris's finest butchers with their racks of fresh meat hanging above their sawdust floors, is now just a part of the city's, new urban developments. Only a few vestiges of its quaint past, like the Pied, now remain.

The loyal patrons of the Pied, when they reach the top of the steep stairs, are invariably greeted there by Francois, its omnipresent maitre d' who they swear must either be identical twins or can defy the laws of physics and be in two places at the same time.

Francois was at the top of the stairs when Mason and Dietz arrived. He greeted them with a smile and led them to a table. Mason sat with his back to the wall; Dietz sat opposite him. The dining room was small and rectangular, its walls and ceiling covered with mirrors. Mason glanced over Dietz's shoulder. Across the room from them was a large obese woman sitting in a double chair the size of a love seat behind several of the small tables that had been pushed together for her. She looked as if she had been lowered behind the tables by a hoist that would have to be used again to lift her out.

Dietz was looking at the menu and discussing it with Francois, who was waiting to take their order. Dietz asked the maitre d' what he recommended. *Que nous conseiliez-vows:"*

Francois smiled. *Le pied de cochon, bien sur!"*

Dietz turned to Mason. "He recommends what the place is named for: the pig's foot. What do you say?"

"I'm willing to give it a try."

Dietz gave Francois their order. *"Alors, du pied de cochon pour deux."*

Francois left and Dietz pushed his chair back from the table.

"I'm going to take a leak. I think I'll enjoy this meal a lot more if I take it now and not wait." He went to look for the men's room.

As soon as Dietz was out of sight, Mason caught Francois's eye and motioned him back to the table. "You are Francois?" *"Oui, monsieur."*

"I'm Steve Mason."

Francois's eyes lit up. "Ah, *Monsieur* Mason! Andre telephoned me about you this afternoon." He stepped closer to the table. "I owe my life to Andre Doucette. There is nothing I would not do for him. He said I might be of assistance to you."

"Do you know a woman named Lisa Helms? I understand she comes here a lot."

Francois smiled. "But of course, Mademoiselle Helms. She had dinner here only last evening "

Mason quickly wrote down the name of his hotel and the telephone number of the Paris Office on a piece of paper. He handed it to Francois. "The next time she makes a reservation, make one for me at the same time, and call me."

Francois slipped the note into his pocket. "I will telephone you right away. Do you want me to arrange for you to be seated next to her?"

Mason thought for a moment. "Yes. But I don't want her to know that I'm interested in her."

Francois smiled. "I understand, ***monsieur."***

Dietz returned. "What was that all about?"

"He was asking about the wine. I told him you were the expert." He handed Dietz the wine list and changed the subject. "I read through the papers you gave me. I think I have a pretty good picture of where we stand. Tomorrow I'd like to take a look at some of your files and check a few notes I made. I want to be ready to deal with this fellow Rijksmeer when we meet him on Saturday."

Dietz had a question. "There's still something I don't understand."

"'What's that?"

"I don't understand how our Sales Managers could go into court and tell the wrong story just because we're shutting down their offices. I mean, they'd be under oath, wouldn't they? What about perjury?"

Mason smiled. "Oh, they wouldn't actually have to lie in a way that we could get them for perjury. All they'd have to do is conveniently forget a few things they'd remember if they wanted to be helpful. I've seen it hundreds of times in cases I've had. And there's not much you can do about it unless you've got them nailed down ahead of time in an affidavit or deposition."

Dietz was impressed. "Where did you go to law school, Steve, Harvard?"

Mason shook his head. "Boston University. I understand you went to school in the States?"

"Yeah, I went to Cal Tech for two years after I graduated from the University of Heidelberg."

"How did you like it our there in California?"

Dietz smiled. "Loved it! Sunshine every day. Lots of beautiful women. It was great!"

Francois returned, took their wine selection, and left. Dietz glanced in the mirror behind Mason. "Holy shit! Take a look behind me at that fat woman sitting across from us. She's just been served an order of oysters you wouldn't believe!"

Mason glanced over Dietz's shoulder. In front of the woman was an enormous pedestal tray heaped with raw oysters, enough for an entire table of people. She was tucking one end of a large napkin under her fat chin and contemplating them with a broad smile Dietz whispered across his palm to Mason. "That's a lot of oysters; there must be three dozen there." He shook his head. "There's no way she's going to eat all those oysters."

They were both watching her now, Mason looking over Dietz's shoulder, Dietz looking in the mirror. The woman, holding a small knife in one hand, took the first oyster off the tray. In one uninterrupted motion, she sliced the oyster out of its shell, slipped it into her mouth, and gulped. She took the empty shell, sucked the juice out of it, ran her tongue around its rough edge, then tossed it back on the tray. She took another oyster and did the same thing. As the second empty shell clattered back on the tray, a third oyster was disappearing into her mouth. The third was followed by a fourth, the fourth by a fifth. She was developing a rhythm now, the oysters following one another like juggler's balls in a smooth continuous circle from the tray to her hand to her mouth, then the empty shell back to the tray again. Dietz shook his head. "Jesus! I never saw anything like that before. How many has she eaten so far?"

Mason kept watching over Dietz's shoulder. "Seven so far—no, wait, there goes number eight."

Dietz laughed. "Let's make a bet. I'll bet you fifty francs she stops on an odd number."

Mason smiled. "You're on. You've got odd; I've got even." He wrote the number eight on his napkin. He glanced over Dietz's shoulder and changed the eight to a nine

Their dinner arrived. Dietz approved the wine and they began eating. Dietz reached into his pocket and took out a piece of paper. "I

Dietz lifted his broken arm out of this lap and rested it on the table. "Great! I'll call Sophie tomorrow and tell her to make a reservation for all of us at the Bali."

Mason changed the number on his napkin to sixteen. "What time is our return flight on Sunday?"

"I made it for late in the day. It's tulip time in Holland and I thought you might like to see the *Keukenhof*"

"What's that?"

"It's a big public park where they have thousands of tulips growing, all crazy kinds. It's quite a take in. I thought we'd go there on our way back to the airport; it's on the way." He pointed his thumb over his shoulder. "How do we stand in the oyster race?"

"She's now up to seventeen."

"Is she slowing down at all?"

Mason watched two more empty shells clatter onto the pedestal tray. "Looks to me like she's just hitting her stride." They both laughed.

By the time they finished dessert and were having coffee, the number on Mason's napkin had climbed to twenty. The tray in front of the woman was now mostly empty shells. Her pace, however, had not slackened; she was still plucking one oyster after another from the pile, slipping it out of its shell into her mouth and tossing the shell back on the tray. Finally, at twenty-eight, she stopped. She poked around in the tray for number twenty-nine but found only empty shells. She gave up and tossed the knife on top of them. She leaned back and wiped her mouth with her napkin.

Dietz took out a fifty franc note and handed it to Mason. "You win, Steve. Holy Jesus! Twenty-eight oysters!" He shook his head. "If I hadn't seen it, I wouldn't believe it."

At the top of the stairs, as they were leaving, Francois stopped them. "You enjoyed your dinners, *messieurs?*"

They both nodded. Dietz pointed to the woman they had been watching "Tell us something. Does that woman come in here and eat oysters like that every time?"

Francois shook his head. "No, no *monsieur.* Sometimes she has escargot or perhaps several pates. She does not have the same appetizer every time."

Mason and Dietz looked at each other and laughed. As they started down the stairs, Mason stopped and reached back to shake

Francois's hand. "I really enjoyed your restaurant. I hope I have a chance to come back soon."

Francois stood at the top of the stairs watching them leave. When they were gone, he looked at what Mason had pressed into his hand. It was a five hundred franc note.

* * *

Lying anesthetized on the stainless steel table in the Hoch laboratory, it did not look like an animal at all. A small ewe, it's entire body had been razor shaved down to the bare pink skin. It looked like a small naked child. A few feet away was a large cylindrical vat filled with a thick yellow liquid. In it were floating glistening silver crystals. Beside the steel table, two men wearing the long white coats of industrial chemists stood waiting. One of them glanced up at the clock on the wall. "It should only be a few more minutes now. Have you called Kopt?"

The other nodded. "He is on his way down." They both bent over the table and examined the animal. It was still under the affect of the drug.

The door to the laboratory opened and Kopt entered. He tapped his cane on the tiled floor. "Well?"

"It is not yet conscious, *Herr Kopt.* But it will only be minute or two now."

Kopt limped to the edge of the vat and looked in. "You are certain this has been prepared according to my specifications?"

"Yes, *Herr Kopt,* everything is precisely as you ordered." One of the chemists pointed to the glistening crystals. "Their appearance is deceptive. They are quiescent now only because they have nothing to react with and are in a stable state. But once—"

Kopt was impatient. "Yes, yes, I know. That is what I am here to see."

The animal on the table moved.

"It is starting to come around now, *Herr Kopt.* In a minute it will be fully conscious."

The ewe stirred; its bare pink skin twitched and it moved its hind legs. Slowly, it raised its head, then rolled over on its stomach and started to get up. One of the chemists reached to hold it down. Kopt waved him away. "Let it get up. Put it on the floor. Let it run around a bit."

On the floor, the animal struggled awkwardly to its feet. Standing up, it was even more obscene. Its entire body, even its head, had been shaved. It just stood there trembling. The chemist prodded it with his foot. "It is fully awake now."

Kopt nodded. "Very well. Bring it over."

The chemist picked it up and carried it to the edge of the vat. In his arms, the animal looked even more like a small child. It began bleating and struggling to get away. Kopt motioned with his head. "All right, do it."

The chemist threw the animal into the vat. It squealed as it fell through the air. It landed with a splash in the yellow liquid and disappeared from sight. Immediately the chemical reaction began, the animal reappeared, squealing with pain as the yellow liquid, now boiling, ate into its bare skin. It thrashed frantically from side to side, only upsetting the crystals more and intensifying the chemical reaction. The crystals, now coated with yellow, hissed even louder, giving off a pungent odor that forced Kopt and the two chemists to hold handkerchiefs to their faces as they watched. The animal, its head and forelegs almost eaten away, clawed pathetically at the smooth wall of the vat. Then the clawing stopped and the animal slid slowly down into the boiling liquid and disappeared. For several minutes, the reaction continued. Then, gradually, it abated and finally stopped. The silver crystals became quiescent again.

Kopt had watched the whole event without expression. For several moments he stood there, not saying anything Then he shook his head. "I am still not satisfied. It is not violent enough; more catalyst is needed." He turned to the chemists. "Prepare another animal."

* * *

The taxi sped smoothly over the highway toward Amsterdam. Mason watched the narrow canals slip by them one after another stretching across the pancake-flat landscape to the horizon. The early morning sun was just beginning to burn the mist off them. The driver had the radio tuned to a rock and roll station and tapping his fingers on the leather dashboard in time with the music.

Mason leaned forward over the front seat. "You sure have a lot of water here."

The driver turned down the music on the radio. "Yes, the sea has always been a big part of our life here in The Netherlands. We have had to struggle against it since the beginning. The airport where you landed is almost twelve feet below sea level." He pointed to the land on both sides of the highway. "At one time, all this belonged to the sea. It is an old polder we reclaimed many years ago. Almost all our country was water originally." He laughed. "We have a saying here in The Netherlands: God created the world, but the Dutch created Holland."

They were now approaching the outskirts of Amsterdam. The houses along the sides of the road were getting closer together, the canals larger and farther apart. The driver pointed out the window again. "That windmill over there is one of the few left that still uses the wind. You can see the new canvas on the sails."

Mason watched out the back window as the windmill receded into the distance behind them. "So, most of them do not use the wind anymore?"

"No, now almost all of them are operated by electrical power."

"And their purpose is just to keep the water moving?"

"That's right. They just keep moving it from one part of the country to the next, then to the next, until they've moved it back to the sea. If they ever stopped, the whole country would be flooded."

Mason was impressed. "That's really something, I mean the way they all work together like that."

The driver smiled. "Yes, and that's another story. In the beginning, when our country was first settled, hundreds of years ago, the early Dutch farmers discovered they could use the wind to keep their land dry. One farmer would put up a windmill to move the water off his land to his neighbor's. His neighbor would do the same, moving the water along to the next piece of land, and so on and so on, until the last one pushed it back out into the sea." He paused. "About twenty years ago, someone in the government came up with the idea that the whole thing should be run by a central water commission. A study was made to see what changes were needed to make it more efficient." He laughed. "Guess what the study showed? That they should leave it alone and not make any changes at all."

Mason smiled. "You mean it was okay the way it was?"

"It was more than that; it was just about perfect. It turned out that the old farmers had set up a system that was as good as we could want; there was no need to change it at all."

Mason laughed and sat back in the seat He looked out the window and could see they were in Amsterdam now. The city was a maze of canals with narrow cobblestone streets on both sides and little humped-back bridges crossing over them. The streets and bridges were crowded with people on bicycles. The houses were tall and thin, jammed together with no space between them, and leaned out at different angles over the street, their ubiquitous hook and pulley at the top for hoisting furniture to the upper floors. They looked as if they had been built from a child's crayon drawing.

The taxi crossed over a humped-back bridge and turned down onto a cobblestone street beside one of the canals. The street was not much wider than the taxi. Mason, looking out the window, could see straight down into the water. He leaned over the driver's shoulder. "How many cars do you have go into the canals?"

The driver laughed. "We fish out about two or three a week. But don't worry, I will not put you in the canal. I am accustomed to driving here in Amsterdam." The taxi turned onto a long bridge over one of the larger canals leading to the harbor. The driver pointed to another bridge off in the distance. "See that other bridge over there, how it is just the same as this one. The one over there was built about ten years ago. The one we are on was built more than three hundred years ago." He laughed. "Another example of how we Dutch think. We decided we had the right idea when we built the first one. We didn't see any reason to change the design when we built the new one."

He crossed the bridge and they were back again in the maze of canals and narrow streets along side them. Mason nudged Dietz as they passed a row of cars parked with their front wheels only inches from the edge of the canal. "I wouldn't' want to get in one of those and make the mistake of starting up in forward and not reverse."

Dietz laughed. "That probably happens a lot, particularly when someone's had a snoot full." He paused. "Oh, by the way, we're meeting this guy Rijksmeer at a hotel called the Schiller. Wait until you see the Schiller; it's a real old Dutch hotel. A friend of mine from Cal Tech stayed there once. He had a funny experience there."

"Oh? What happened?"

"Well, as I understand it, the rooms in old Dutch hotels don't normally have showers in them. The Schiller had a few, though, and my friend paid extra to get one they said had a shower in it. The shower turned out to be just a metal stall built onto the outside of the building." Dietz laughed. "They must have just knocked a hole in the wall, and hung the thing there. Anyway, when my friend was there, it was winter. He found the metal stall unheated and cold as a bastard. But he'd made up his mind he was going to take a shower, so he got in and turned on the water."

Mason guessed what Dietz was going to tell him. know, there was no hot water."

"No, the water was hot enough. There was no soap. There he was, standing under the shower, all wet and bare ass, and there was not soap. He got out of the shower and looked around the room, but there was no soap anywhere. He was mad as hell. He put all his clothes on again and stormed downstairs to the lobby. He marched up to the desk clerk and said "Where the hell is my soap?"

"What did the clerk say?"

"Nothing He just smiled and handed him a cake of soap. Its the custom in old Dutch hotels not to put any soap in the room. If you want soap, you're supposed to ask for it at the desk when you register."

"They both laughed.

The driver turned right at the next corner, pulled over to the side of the street and stopped. "Well, gentlemen, here we are at your hotel, the Amstel."

Dietz turned to Mason. "It's just eight o'clock. How about, after we check in, we meet again in the lobby in half an hour. That'll give us plenty of time to get over to the Schiller by nine

Mason nodded. "Fine. I want to hit the head anyway. I haven't had my morning constitutional yet."

* * *

Mason put his briefcase on the table beside the bed and looked at his watch. It was 6:10. The meeting with Rijksmeer had gone well, he thought. Dietz was right; the Dutchman was a key player in the lawsuit It had taken them all day in the windowless conference room at the Schiller to get into an affidavit what Rijksmeer could tell them about Chimique's operations in Holland. When they were finished, Rijksmeer insisted on taking them into the Schiller bar. By the time the public secretary had typed up the affidavit for the Dutchman to sign, they had all had several drinks. Rijksmeer wanted everyone to stay and have dinner with him. When Mason and Dietz declined, he invited the public secretary anyway.

Mason opened his briefcase, took out Rijksmeer's affidavit, and glanced through it. It was more than twenty pages long. One thing was certain, he decided, the guy had no idea Hoch was planning to close his office. Mason slipped the affidavit back in his briefcase. He felt a little guilty about how they were deceiving the Dutchman, particularly after Dietz laid it on so heavy about Hoch's having plans for expanding the Amsterdam office.

Mason hung his jacket over one of the chairs. He kicked off his shoes, loosened his tie, and lay down on the bed. He put his hands behind his head, closed his eyes, and took stock. So far, so good, he thought; the cover story seemed to be working; everyone was convinced he was over here to work on Hoch's case against Chimique. He smiled to himself Running into Doucette was certainly a break. Thanks to Doucette's contact at the Pied, he was now set to meet Lisa when she had dinner there again. He frowned. He had to be careful, though, that he didn't blow it right at the beginning If he did, the whole thing would go down the tube. He had to be careful not to rush things; that was important. Everything depended on his getting close to her without making her suspicious. After that, he would still have to get her to trust him enough to tell him where her father was. It was a tall order and wasn't going to be easy. How to do it all was still a big question. He rubbed the back of his neck with this clasped hands. There were other nagging questions too. Why was Kopt so mysterious? What had Molte done that made him so important to the Israelis? And who was the guy in the gray vest; what was his role in all of this? There were a lot of questions and no answers. He opened his eyes, got up and walked across the room to the writing table. He sat down, took a sheet of the Amstel's stationery, and wrote a long letter to Joanne.

* * *

The Queen Wilhelmina was one of Amsterdam's shabby little hotels that survived only because of the city's flourishing drug culture. It had little to commend it: the rooms were in need of paint and repair; the hallways and toilets were covered with graffiti, the patrons were alcoholics, drug abusers, and unlicensed prostitutes.

To Seig, however, it had a redeeming feature: the front room he had rented on the top floor offered an unobstructed view across the *Maurigraclit* to the red-carpeted entrance to the Amstel. From it he had watched Mason arrive at the hotel that morning He had seen him leave a half hour later and had followed him to the Schiller. Back now at the window, he was waiting for Mason to come out for the evening. Behind him on the bed was the black leather case he would take with him when he followed Mason this time. He had already checked its contents. Everything was there: the custom made Mauser, the silencer, and, if distance should be a factor, the specially designed shoulder piece and telescopic sight. He looked across the *Maurigracht* at the Amstel again. The early evening parade of people coming out to their taxis was beginning It would not be long now, he thought. He moved his chair closer to the window and waited.

As they stepped out onto the red carpet in front of the hotel, Dietz commented what a nice spring evening it was and suggested they walk to where they were meeting the two women. "Besides, Steve, it will give you a chance to see some of the city along the way."

Mason found the walk enjoyable. Dietz showed him the historic *Munt Tower,* then took him down the famous *Kalverstraat,* to Dam Square. "This is where the city started, where they first dammed up the old Amstel River." He stopped at a large war monument in the center of the square. "This was once called "Hippy Haven." Back in the sixties, before the government finally did something about it, the whole monument swarmed with hundreds of hippies, all dirty and drugged up, using it as a place to hang out all day, then sleeping on it all night. It was a mess."

"What did the government do about it?

"Well, the Dutch pride themselves in being liberal and tolerant of other people's lifestyles, so they did not want to start knocking heads or anything like that. What they decided to do was start a program of cleaning the old monument. Every afternoon, government workers would show up with sandblasters, scrub brushes and soap. Then at the end of the day, the fire department would come and hose the whole thing down. The hippies had to get off while it was being sandblasted and scrubbed, and when they came back to settle in for the night, the whole thing was wet, with puddles everywhere. They weren't being told they couldn't sleep there, and they couldn't complain that the government wanted to clean its monument. It worked; the hippies finally gave up and went somewhere else."

Dietz took Mason across Dam Square to the front of the Hotel Krasnapolsky. Beside the hotel was a narrow street marked *Pijisteeg.* Dietz started down the street and motioned for Mason to follow. Halfway down the street they came to a wooden door over which was hanging a painted sign with the words *Wijnand Fockink.* On both sides of the door were smoked glass windows. Through them, Mason could see the place was packed with people. Dietz cradled his broken arm up close to his chest, and pushed his way in. Mason followed him.

The place was small and wall-to-wall with people standing crowded together, talking loudly, drinking and laughing. All around the room were high wooden shelves, sagging with age, on which were old dusty, odd shaped casks. At one end of the room was a low wooden bar, only slightly higher than Mason's knees. Behind it, two buxom barmaids wearing Dutch costumes were serving drinks and joking with the customers. Dietz looked around. "I don't see Sophie. I guess they're not here yet. Let's have a drink while we're waiting. Have you ever had a *Jenever,* Steve?"

"No, what is it?"

"It's the traditional Dutch drink." He pulled Mason over to the bar and caught the eye of one of the baimaids. *"Twee Jenever, ulsiublieft:"*

"Jong of oud?"

"Twee ottd."

Dietz smiled. "They have two kinds, Steve, young and old. I ordered the old; it's stronger."

The barmaid put two tulip-shaped glasses on the low bar. Then, taking a large flask full of what looked to Mason like gin, she carefully filled them to the very brim. Dietz laughed. "That's the custom here. They fill them up like that so you can't pick them up without spilling them. You have to slurp them first. Here, watch this." He bent over the bar, sticking out his rear end so it pushed the person behind him out of the way, and sipped one of the glasses with a loud slurping noise. He straightened up again and smiled. "Okay, Steve, your turn."

Mason bent over and did the same thing The jenever tasted a little like gin but was different somehow. He liked it. He picked up the glasses, handed one to Dietz, and they both stepped away from the bar to make room for someone else. Mason watched, smiling, as other customers, in turn, bent over the bar to slurp their *jenevers,* all sticking their rear ends out and pushing the people behind them out of the way. Everyone seemed to take the custom in good humor.

Mason noticed in one corner of the room a young man and woman wearing denim jackets and tight jeans leaning against each other, their faces nuzzled together, oblivious to what was going on around them. The girl, an olive-skinned Surinamese, was pressed up against the wall by her companion,—a short, husky Dutch youth with stringy blond hair and an unkempt beard. She had her hand on his and was holding it between her legs. Her other hand was draped over his shoulder, her fingers playing with the back of his neck. Mason saw that Dietz was looking toward the door. "What time did you tell them we'd be here?"

"I said we'd meet them here at seven-thirty. It's only a few minutes after that now. Want to have anotherjenever?"

"Sure."

As they started toward the bar, Dietz stopped. "There they are, Steve, they just came in. The one on the left, the one with the big boobs, is Sophie." He laughed. I think she's got the biggest pair in Amsterdam. The other one is her friend, Karin."

Mason smiled. It was easy to tell which one was Sophie. The shorter and heavier of the two, she was wearing a tight red sweater and a leather jacket that would have been impossible to button had she wanted to. Her friend, Karin, was a contrast: tall and thin, almost skinny, with curly blond hair and big round eyes that seemed to be expressing constant surprise.

Dietz brought the two women over to where Mason was standing. "Sophie, Karin, this is my friend, Steve Mason." Mason smiled. "It's nice to meet you both."

Sophie pointed to Dietz's cast. "What did you do to your arm,
Carl?"

Dietz laughed. "Something stupid. I tried to show the experts at Grenoble how to ski, and ended up hitting a tree. It's broken in three places."

"It looks uncomfortable."

"Oh, I'm getting used to it now." He smiled. "But don't worry; it doesn't prevent me from doing the important things like *zoals met jouw naar bed gaan.*"

Sophie laughed. "I'm sure it would take more than a broken arm to do that!"

Dietz pushed his way up to the bar again. "What would you girls like to drink? Steve and I are having *jenevers, oud.*"

"We'll have the same."

Dietz caught the barmaid's eye. *Vier jenevers, alstublieft.*"

The barmaid put four of the tulip-shaped glassed on the bar and filled them to the brim. Mason, Dietz, Sophie, and Karin took turns bending over and slurping them, sticking out their rear ends while the others laughed. Out of the corner of his eye, Mason could see the young man and woman in the corner. They were still at it, his hand between her legs, his thumb now slowly rubbing the seam of her jeans. Her eyes were glassy and she was biting her lower lip.

Deitz drew Sophie off to one side so Mason and Karin could get acquainted. Karin broke the ice. "Sophie tells me you are a lawyer."

"That's right."

"Do you go into court a lot?"

"Not as much as I used to, but still a lot. I understand you're still going to school."

"Yes, I'm a graduate student at the engineering school in Delft. I'm studying civil engineering."

Mason pointed around the room. "This is quite a place. It looks like it was something else once."

"It was. It's called *a proeflokaal,* which means tasting place. At one time it was where people came to buy wines and spirits. The wines and spirits were kept in those old casks you see on the shelves there. The custom was to let people taste samples from them before they bought anything. After a while, the proprietor realized too many people were coming in just to taste and talk, and not buy anything

So, he started charging them for what they drank. But it's still called a tasting place."

Mason saw she had finished *her jenever.* He pointed to her glass. Would you like another?"

She looked at him. "Will you slurp it for me?"

Mason laughed. "Sure." He motioned the barmaid for two more *jenevers,* slurped them both, then handed one to Karin.

He heard Dietz whisper in his ear. "Have you been watching those two in the corner. I think he's going to bring her off, if he hasn't already. I'm getting horny just watching them." He laughed, then turned to Sophie and Karin. "Well, let's finish this last *borrel,* and go. I promised old Steve here a *rijsttafel.* He's never had one."

Karin put her hand on Mason's arm. "Oh, you'll enjoy it, Steve. It's really fun."

They finished their drinks and left.

* * *

The Indonesian maitre d' at the Bali bowed as they entered. Dietz was right; the place was reminiscent of a Chinese restaurant, but different somehow. The maitre d' seated them at a long narrow table, Dietz and Sophie on one side, Mason and Karin on the other. Their chairs were close together and Mason could feel his leg touching Karin's. Dietz called over the maitre d' and let Sophie deal with him in Dutch. Karin translated for Mason. "The waiter is asking if we want a drink. beforehand. Sophie is telling him yes, but that with the meal we all want beer. She is right; some of the dishes are very hot and it is best to have something to put out the fire." She put her hand on Mason's arm. "There is a lot to eat, Steve, and you must at least try everything. Taste a little of everything first; then take more of what you like the most."

They all decided to have another *jenever* and Sophie ordered the meal at the same time. Mason was conscious of his leg still touching Karin's. He thought about moving it away but did not.

They had barely finished their drinks when suddenly they were surrounded by a host of Indonesian waiters in white jackets scurrying back and forth, arranging a row of small metal stands down the middle of the table like a train of flatbed railroad cars. Under each one they placed a small lighted candle. One of the waiters said something to Mason. "*Voorzichtig* **meneer, de platen zyn heet."**

Karin squeezed Mason's arm. "He says be careful; the stands become very hot and will burn you if you touch them."

Once the small stands were all in place, the waiters paraded in with one dish after another until the whole table was covered with food. Then one of them stood at the center of the table and explained in Dutch what each dish contained. Karin again translated for Mason.

That dish he just pointed to is ***bakjang;*** its stuffed rice wrapped in banana leaves. The next one is ***kepiting,*** a sort of crab dish that's one of my favorites." The waiter pointed to one of the sauces, said something and smiled. Karin laughed and squeezed Mason's arm. "He says if you take too much of that, you'll go blind." They both laughed.

The ***rijsttafel*** was everything Dietz had promised, and then some. Mason had never tasted so many different exotic things, all of them delicious. Sophie ordered a second round of beer and to Mason's amazement they finished all the food on the table. Dietz turned to Sophie and Karin. "What do you say, after we leave here, we take old Steve to see the *Walletjes?*"

The two women laughed and Karin turned to Mason. "The *Walletj es* is another name for our red light district here in Amsterdam. But it's okay to go there early like this; it's a fun place to see; it's really sort of a tourist attraction."

Mason nodded. "I'm ready."

Dietz called for the bill. As they all got up, Mason reached over and took Karin's hand.

* * *

The ***Walletjes,*** located in the oldest section of Amsterdam near the railroad station, is not far from the Bali, and they decided to walk rather than bother with a taxi.

It was easy for Mason to tell when they were there. The place had the same little cobblestone streets and canals characteristic of Amsterdam, but now everywhere on both sides of the street, in store front windows, were women sitting in provocative poses, some naked with their legs crossed, others wearing only flimsy negligees that left nothing to the imagination, a few in kinky outfits to attract customers with special fetishes. Behind every one of them was a small cozy room with a bed, the covers turned down, and little red lamp giving everything inside a warm intimate glow.

To Mason, the women all had a sameness about them, sitting there like statues with bored expressions, every now and then catching the eye of a passer-by, giving him a smile and a nod of invitation, then becoming a statue again. In some of the rooms the lights were on but the curtains were drawn. Not all of the invitations were being ignored.

Dietz was walking with his arm draped over Sophie's shoulder, his hand resting casually on one of her large breasts. She had her arm around his waist. Mason and Karin were walking behind them, Karin still holding Mason's hand. Mason turned to her and smiled. "I have to admit, Karin, I've seen a few red light districts before, but this place is something different. See, over there, that old couple just strolling along looking in the windows like they were in a shopping mall. And there, right behind them, that whole family with kids." He laughed. "You were right; the place is a tourist attraction."

Karin pointed to one of the windows where the curtain was drawn. "Yes, but as you can see, not all who come here are tourists."

They stopped at the next corner to wait for the traffic light to change. Dietz drew Mason aside. "Look, Steve, I'm going to take Sophie home; I won't be back to the hotel tonight. It's okay with Karin; Sophie already told her we might be leaving you two alone." He paused. "You're getting along all right with Karin, aren't you?"

Mason nodded. "Don't worry about us, Carl; you and Sophie go ahead."

Dietz gave Mason a friendly punch on the arm. "Okay, I'll see you at the hotel tomorrow morning about ten."

Sophie put her hand out to Mason. "It's been nice meeting you, Steve; I hope you can come back to Amsterdam before your business over here is finished."

Mason shook her hand. "Maybe I will. Anyway, it's been nice meeting you. I really enjoyed the *rijstiafel.*"

Dietz and Sophie climbed into a taxi and drove off When they were gone, Karin turned to Mason. "If you've seen enough of this place, Steve, I do not live far from here; we can walk there and have another jenever if you'd like."

Mason gave her shoulder a gentle squeeze. "I'd like that" He smiled at her. "I'll even slurp yours for you."

They had only walked a short distance when they were out of the red light district and in a section of the city where the streets were quiet and deserted. Mason had his arm around Karin and she was leaning on his shoulder. They stopped on one of the humped-back bridges to drop some pebbles into the dark water below, then continued across the bridge and along the side of the canal. Karin looked up at Mason. "This street we're on was once the most famous in Amsterdam."

Mason looked at her. "What's the name of it?"

"Kloveniersburgwal."

Mason laughed. "That's a mouthful, even for a Dutch word. What does it mean?"

"It means Street of the Diamond Cutters. This is where they all had their shops, here along this street." Karin pointed to the buildings around them, all dark and deserted. "But that was long ago; they are all gone; there is nothing here now but old warehouses."

They had walked several yards from the bridge when Mason suddenly stopped.

"What's the matter, Steve?"

"Look up there, ahead of us."

Between them and the next bridge, a car with its headlights turned off had just pulled into the middle of the street and stopped, blocking their way. Two men got out and were walking toward them. Mason took his arm from around Karin's shoulder. "I don't like the look of this. Let's get the hell out of here." As they turned to go back, Mason's eyes narrowed. A second car was sealing off the other end of the street. fle grabbed Karin's hand and they started running back to the footbridge they had just crossed. They had almost reached it when a man climbed out of the second car and stood in their way.

He was a big man, as tall as Mason but much heavier. His head was covered with a tight nylon stocking that distorted his face into an ugly mask. Through the nylon his thick lips snarled at them. Karin screamed and grabbed Mason's arm. "Oh God! They're Moluccans!"

The man snarled again and raised a heavy object over his head. It caught the streetlight and Mason saw it was a meat cleaver. He shook Karin's hands off his arm and pushed her in back of him. He remembered now reading somewhere that an elderly couple had been hacked to death in Amsterdam by some Moluccan terrorists. He glanced up the street and saw the two other men getting closer. He tried to reason with the one blocking his way. "Look, fella, why don't you put that thing down; we're just on our way to—" Karin screamed as the man swung at Mason with the cleaver. Mason ducked and the thick blade just missed his head. He reached in his pocket quickly and took out his wallet. "Here, here's my money." The man snarled and raised his arm again. Mason, keeping his eye on the cleaver, held the wallet out a little more. "Here, take it; it's all the money I've got." The eyes behind the nylon shifted back and forth, then focused on the wallet. The man put his hand out to take it but it was just out of his reach. He motioned for Mason to come closer. Mason held the wallet out a little further. It was now only inches from the man's hand. "Here, take it; you can have it." The man hesitated, then took a step forward to grab it. The step forward was what Mason was waiting for. He dropped the wallet and grabbed the man's outstretched arm. Spinning in fast and low, and snapping the arm down sharply over his shoulder, he swept his right leg back up in an arabesque as high as he could. He felt his leg catch the man's thick inner thigh. It was not a good ***uchi mata;*** but it was good enough. The cleaver clattered on the cobblestones as the man went upside down over Mason's back. He cart wheeled though the air and down into the canal with a splash. Mason grabbed Karin's hand and they ran across the bridge. They reached the other side and cut through a narrow alley to the next canal. In the distance they could see the lights of the ***Walletjes.*** They ran towards it.

The Moluccan was just climbing out of the canal when his two companions, carrying cleavers, rushed up to him. They argued for a moment about what to do, then started across the bridge. They were halfway across when they saw the figure standing at the other end, smoking a cigarette and waiting for them. They raised their cleavers and rushed at him.

As the three men came towards him, Seig took his hand out of his topcoat. The first shot from the Mauser hit the Moluccan who had fallen in the canal, the soft-nosed bullet making a small hole in the front of his wet nylon stocking, then taking the back of his head off. The next two shots, almost simultaneous, were chest shots that dropped the other Moluccans like stones only a few yards from the end of the bridge. Sieg slipped the Mauser back into his topcoat. He threw away his cigarette, dragged the three bodies to the side of the bridge, and rolled them off into the canal. He picked up the three cleavers and threw them in as well. He decided it was no use trying to find Mason now. He lit another cigarette, then headed back to the Wilhelmina.

The red light district was still crowded but had changed; there were fewer tourists and more customers. Mason saw that Karen was still trembling. "Hey, listen, we're safe now."

She buried her head in his chest. "I know; I just can't seem to stop."

Mason put his arm around her. "What do you say, kid, are you still up to a little *jenever* slurping?"

Karin lifted her head off his chest and kissed him on the mouth.

* * *

Mason unrolled the large poster he had bought in Holland. . He held it at arm's length and looked at it. It was a picture of the knolls at the *Keukenhof* covered with bright colored tulips of all different sizes and shapes. He smiled. It captured the essence of the place, he thought. He tacked it on the wall of his office, stepped back and looked at it again. He frowned. It was crooked. He was still looking at it when Nadine, the petite secretary he shared with Dietz, came in. She glanced at the poster. "It is not straight, *monsieur.*"

Mason put his hands on her shoulders, marched her across the room to the front of his desk, and positioned her there. "Stand right here, Nadine." He walked back to the poster and adjusted it. "How's this?"

"Yes, that is better."

He walked back and sat down at his desk. "Well, Nadine, what do you have for me this morning?"

She consulted her note pad. "The file you were looking for; *Monsieur* Dietz has it."

"Okay, I'll get it from him. What else?"

She looked again at her note pad. ***"Monsieur*** Doucette called and said he had a message for you from someone named Francois."

Mason leaped up from his chair "Great! Get a hold of Doucette right away. Tell him I'd like to see him. I'll be in the next office with Dietz."

Mason found the Hoch engineer pouring over a complicated blueprint spread out on his desk. He had one end anchored under the telephone; the other he was holding down by resting his cast on it. He looked up as

Mason came in his office. "You know, Steve, I've been studying this Chimique flow diagram for about an hour now. It's nothing but a Chinese copy of ours."

Mason looked over Dietz's shoulder at the blueprint. "We'll need an independent expert to testify to that, but we shouldn't have any problem on that score. And being able to show what you say will help our case a lot." He glanced around the room. "Nadine said you have the sales managers file. Are you using it?"

Dietz shook his head. "No. I was, but I'm finished with it." He reached under the blueprint and produced the file. "I was checking to see who we should meet with next."

"What do you think?"

Dietz shrugged his shoulders as he handed Mason the file. "I don't think if makes much difference, so long as it's one of the next five or six on the list there. You got any ideas?"

Mason looked at the list. "I think the guy in London should be next. His office covers the whole U.K., and Hoch is getting a lot of competition from Chimique there."

"Okay, I'll get in touch with him and set up a meeting."

Outside in the hall someone coughed. Doucette appeared at the door all out of breath. It was obvious he had hurried from wherever he had been. You wanted to see me right away, *Monsieur* Mason?"

"Yes, but let's go to my office where we won't disturb Carl here." He handed the sales manager file back to Dietz.

When they were back in Mason's office, Mason motioned for Doucette to have a seat, then closed the door. "I understand you've heard from Francois?"

Doucette, still out of breath, waddled over to one of the chairs and sat down. He took out a handkerchief and wiped his forehead. "Yes, *monsiuer*, while you were in Amsterdam. He could not reach you at your hotel, so he telephoned me. He said the person you spoke to him about has made a reservation for this Thursday. She is going to have dinner alone. He has reserved a table for you at nine o'clock."

Mason reached over his desk and pumped Doucette's hand. "Andre, you really came through! I can't tell you what this is all about, but you've been a great help. Thanks "

Doucette stuffed his handkerchief back in his trousers, half of it still sticking out of this pocket. "I'm pleased to be of assistance, ***monsieur.***" He noticed the poster on the wall. "I see you went to the ***Keukenhof*** while you were in Holland."

"Yes, Dietz and I went there yesterday. Have you ever been there?"

Doucette shook his head. "No. Except for a brief period during the war, I have never been outside France."

For a few moments, neither of them said anything. Then Doucette leaned forward. "This woman at the Pied, it is important to you that you meet her, is it not? I do not mean to pry, ***monsieur,*** but I sense that it is."

Mason was surprised by Doucette's directness. He hesitated, then nodded. "You're right, Andre, it is."

Doucette continued to lean forward. "You must forgive me, *monsieur;* I speak this way only because I want to be of whatever service I can."

"You've already been a big help, Andre."

"You mean by speaking to Francois?" Doucette shrugged his narrow shoulders. "That was nothing, *monsieur;I* am capable of much more if you need it."

Mason stood up. "Thanks, Andre, but I think I can manage things from here on." He smiled. "I appreciate the offer, though."

After Doucette left, Mason told Nadine to hold his calls, and again shut the door to his office. He unlocked the bottom drawer of his desk and took out the small attache case he had brought from Boston. He put it on his desk, spun the numbers of the little combination lock, and opened it. In it were the photographs of Lisa Helms Kopt had given him. For several minutes he sat studying them. She was certainly beautiful; there was no question about that. And from what Kopt said, she was just as intelligent. Getting close to her was not going to be easy. Yet everything depended on his doing just that. He would not be the first one to try to get around her; and if he screwed up he would be like all the others before who had failed. The key was to get off on the right foot; more importantly not get off on the wrong one. He had to be careful she did not suspect anything If she did, it would be all over; he would have blown the whole thing right at the start. He put the photographs back in the attache case, spun his chair around, and stared out the window at the roof of the building next door. He had to figure out some way to break the ice with her. The ideal thing would be to have something happen so they got to know each other by accident, something even he did not know was going to happen. He sat for several minutes thinking about the problem. Then suddenly an idea flashed into his mind. He spun his chair back to the desk, picked up the telephone and dialed. "Hello, Andre? It's Steve Mason again. Have you got another few minutes? I think I may need your help after all."

. The words CHASE MANHATTAN BANK OF NEW YORK seemed out of place in the midst of all the French names on the other commercial buildings on the *Rue Cambon*. Mason paused briefly on the sidewalk, then went in. The bank was crowded with students in denim jackets and jeans waiting at the teller's cages to cash checks from home. He walked past them and sat down beside the desk of one of the bank officers. The man at the desk looked up.

"Oui, monsieur?"

"Do you speak English?

The man responded flatly. "Yes, of course."

Mason produced the letter of credit Kopt had given him. "I want to draw on this."

The bank officer looked at the letter of credit, then at Mason. "Certainly, *monsieur.*" He forced a smile, trying to appear friendly. "If you do not mind my saying so, *monsieur*, this is a very liberal letter of credit. How much do you wish to draw?"

"I want a bank check in the amount of 276,884 francs, made payable to *Jacques St. Marie Porsche Distributeurs.*" Mason took a slip of paper out of his pocket and handed to him. "Here's the full name and address."

The bank officer asked Mason to sign the letter of credit, then took it and left. He returned in a few minutes with the check. He handed it to Mason with another forced smile. "It must be a very fine car you are buying, ***monsieur.***"

Mason took the check and stuffed it in his pocket. "I guess it is.

I haven't seen it yet."

* * *

Albert liked his job. His pay for parking cars at the Pied was modest but the position had its perks: they gave him a uniform with the restaurant's name on it; he got to drive all the fancy cars he saw in the magazines; and when he brought the patrons their cars after dinner, he would usually get slipped a few francs. Not a bad job, he told himself. He looked at his watch. It was quarter to nine. He glanced up the *Rue Coquillere* and smiled. The evening ahead was going to be interesting, he thought. None of it made any sense to him. But Francois had told him exactly what to do; and he could use the extra francs he had been promised if everything went right. He looked up the street again.

Mason was just getting the hang of the four speed shift in his new Porsche when he reached the *Rue Coquillere*. He down shifted and, hardly touching the brake pedal, brought the car to a smooth stop in front of the Pied. He turned off the motor and got out.

Albert was standing there waiting. "*Bonsoir!* You are *Monsieur* Mason, *n'est pas?*"

Mason was surprised the parking attendant knew his name. "Yes, Pm Mr. Mason.'

Albert smiled. "I am Albert. I will take your car to the garage. The maitre d', Francois will tell me when you have finished dinner, and I will have it here for you then."

Mason handed him the keys and went up the steep stairs to the restaurant.

Albert stood for a moment admiring the new Porsche. Then, shaking his head, he got in and drove it around to the garage.

Francois greeted Mason at the top of the stairs. "Ah. ***Monsieur*** Mason!"

"Hello, Francois."

The maitre d' tucked a large menu under his arm and led Mason to a corner of the dining room where two small tables were reserved. He waited until Mason was seated at one of them, then handed him the menu. "You are fortunate to have a reservation, ***monsieur;*** we are fully booked tonight."

Mason ordered a kir to drink while he looked at the menu. Francois was right; except for Mason's table and the one next to it, all the others were taken. The restaurant had twice as many customers as the week before. He smiled, wondering how many were Doucette's relatives.

Mason nursed his kir and continued to study the menu while he waited for Lisa to show up. He tried to keep an eye on the entrance to the dining room but it was not until she was standing right next to him, waiting for Francois to pull out her table for her, that he saw she had arrived. His eyes widened at the sight of her. She had on a white jacket with matching vest and skirt, and was wearing a bright red blouse, unbuttoned at the top, that emphasized her long sensual neck. The photographs Kopt gave him did not do her justice; she had to be one of the most beautiful women he had ever seen. Their tables were close together and as she squeezed in between them to sit down, she brushed against him. *"Excusez-moi, monsieur."* When she was seated, she took a small note pad from her handbag and placed it on the table. She glanced at the menu, discussed it briefly with Francois in French, then ordered.

The maitre d' bowed. *"Tres bien, mademoiselle."* He turned to Mason. "Have you decided, *monsieur?"*

Mason handed Francois his menu. "I'll have whatever she's having." He saw out the corner of his eye he had made Lisa smile.

He turned to her. "Would you like to share a bottle of wine? But only if you pick it and I pay for it."

She hesitated. "But I may select something you do not like."

Mason shrugged. "Whatever you say is okay with me. After all, we're both having the same thing." He smiled. "By the way, what did we order?"

She laughed. ***"Ratatouille Nicose."*** It is quite good here." She paused. "I mean if you like ***ratatouille."***

"I'm sure I'll like it." He stuck out his hand. "My name is Steve Mason."

She shook his hand. "I'm Lisa Helms. Is this your first time at the Pied?"

"I was here once before, last week. I liked it and decided to come back."

Lisa ordered the wine, then turned to Mason. "Can I ask you a question?"

"Go ahead."

"Do you always have what someone else has?"

"I do when I'm in a French restaurant and the someone else is French and a regular customer of the place."

"But how do you know I am a regular customer?"

Mason laughed. "Oh, that's easy; the way you talk to the maitre d', it's obvious you come here often."

She nodded. "Well, you're right; I am what I suppose you would call a regular customer. I do come here quite often. But you are wrong about my being French. I am Gelman."

"Well, you could have fooled me, I mean the way you speak French." He leaned over and whispered. "Actually, I'm not French either." They both laughed.

Francois returned with the wine. He opened the bottle and hesitated. Mason pointed at Lisa's glass. "She'll do the honors."

Lisa tasted the wine and nodded her approval. As Francois filled their glasses, she turned to Mason. "You are an American?"

Mason smiled. "It shows, huh?" She nodded and Mason laughed. "Yes, I'm a lawyer from Boston, Massachusetts, a trial lawyer."

"Sounds exciting."

"Sometimes it is, although it's not as glamorous as they make it appear on television." He paused. "What do you do for a living?"

"I write articles for a newspaper."

"What kind of articles?"

"All kinds."

"Do you just write about anything you want?"

"Pretty much, yes. Sometimes, of course, I—" She interrupted herself "Ah, here is dinner."

While they were eating, Mason noticed Lisa kept pausing now and then to make a note on the small pad of paper beside her plate. He turned to her. "Are you making notes for an article you're writing?"

She shook her head. "No, Pm just jotting down some thoughts for a talk I have to give this week-end."

"On writing?"

"Actually it is on sculpturing."

"Oh?"

"It is just to a small group of students at the *Jeu de Paume*. The museum is having a special exhibition this month, and I have been asked to take part in it."

"Is it open to the public, your talk, I mean?"

Lisa laughed. "Yes, I suppose it is. But I do not expect anyone other than the students to be interested in what I have to say."

Their conversation was interrupted by Francois who hurried over to them, clearly upset about something.

"Pardonnez-moi, mademoiselle et monsieur, je suis—" He stopped and looked at Mason. "Oh, of course, I should speak English. I am afraid there has been an accident in our parking garage. No one was injured but damage was done to some of the automobiles. Unfortunately, both of yours were involved. I do not know yet the extent of the damage, and of course the Pied will take care of any repairs required. But I must ask you both to come to the garage with me to confirm the damage for insurance purposes. I promise you will not be detained any longer than absolutely necessary."

Lisa stuffed her note pad back in her handbag. "Damn! I hope my car is not badly damaged. I am planning to drive to Germany next week and—" She stopped and looked at Mason. "Oh, *monsieur,* how selfish of me! I hope your car is not badly damaged either."

Mason shrugged. "Well, these things do happen."

Albert was there waiting for them in the garage. He led them to the elevator, chattering excitedly in French to Francois. Mason turned to Lisa. "What's he saying?"

She frowned. "He keeps saying it was an accident and not his fault. He says one of the cars is only damaged a little."

"Does he say which one?"

She shook her head. "No. He just keeps repeating that he is a very careful driver. I think he is worried about losing his job."

In the elevator, Francois gave them a brief report of the accident. "Apparently, *mademoiselle,* when the attendant was parking your car, his foot slipped off the brake and on to the accelerator, causing your car to back into *Monsieur* Mason's. I am afraid, *Monsieur* Mason, that it smashed the headlights of your car."

They stepped out of the elevator and followed Albert across the garage to where the accident occurred. Lisa's car, a small red Renault, was hardly damaged at all. The rear bumper was dented and there were traces of white paint on it; that was all. The major damage had been done to the front of Mason's Porsche. Both headlights were broken and there was glass all over the floor. Lisa turned to Mason. "What a beautiful car! It looks brand new."

Mason nodded. "I bought it yesterday."

Lisa made a face. "Only yesterday! Oh, what a shame!"

Francois pointed to the Renault. "The damage to your car, *mademoiselle,* appears to be slight. It should not be too much trouble to repair. If you will just send me the bill—"

Lisa stopped him. "There's so little damage, Francois, I will probably not bother with it. I am more concerned about what my car has done to *Monsieur* Mason's."

Mason bent down and examined the Porsche. "I'm sure it can be fixed." He looked up at Francois. "But I don't see how I can drive it without headlights."

The maitre d' nodded. "Yes, that is a problem. It will have to be taken somewhere to be repaired. But you are right; you cannot drive it tonight. Where are you staying, *monsieur?* I will call a taxi to take you there."

"The Pont Royal. But don't bother. I'll go out and catch one on the street."

Francois protested. "No, no, *monsieur.* I would not think of having you stand on the street. I will go back to the Pied and call one for you. They are sometimes a bit slow in coming at this hour but—"

Lisa seemed relieved. "Yes, maybe it is only my imagination." She stayed on the ***Quai Voltaire*** until it reached the ***Rue de Bac,*** then took the ***Rue de Bac*** to the ***Rue Montelalbert.*** She turned down the short ***Rue Montelalbert*** and pulled up in front of the Pont Royal. "Well, Steve, here we are at your hotel."

Mason glanced out the back window again. The Mercedes had followed them the whole way. It was stopped at the beginning of the ***Rue***

Montelalbert, waiting. Mason turned to Lisa. "Hey, do me a favor, will you?" She looked at him but did not say anything. He pointed with his thumb back over his shoulder. "That guy who was behind us is still there. I don't think he's following you but—" He paused. "But just in case he is, when I get out I'll wait on the sidewalk while you drive off. You watch in your rear view mirror. If he starts up and follows you, drive around the block and come right back here. Will you do that?"

She hesitated for a moment, then nodded. Mason stuck out his hand and smiled. "Well, if I'm right and he's not following you, I guess this is good night. Thanks a lot for the lift." He shook her hand and got out.

As she drove off, Mason looked back at the Mercedes. It had pulled over to the curb and turned off its lights. Mason was relieved. He ran out into the middle of the street and waved good-bye to Lisa just as she was turning the corner toward the ***Rue de Bac*** again As her Renault disappeared, he heard its little horn beep back to him.

There was no light on in the call girl's apartment. She was either asleep or still out, Mason thought. He smiled to himself Or maybe she was performing in the dark. He looked down to the street. The Mercedes was gone. It had been old Gray Vest again, no doubt about that. Mason bit his lip. Sometime I'm going to confront the bastard and find out why he's going through all this shadowing routine anyway. I'd like to know who the hell is paying him. He sat down at the writing table, took a sheet of paper from the drawer, and wrote out a telex to Arthur Sawyer at the Chase Manhattan Bank in New York.

FOLLOWING IS MESSAGE FOR G.KOPT:

WORKING HARD ON ASSIGNMENT IN HOCH V. CHIMIQUE. EVERYONE HERE CONVINCED IMPORTANCE OF CASE. LIFE NOT ALL WORK THOUGH. HAD DINNER TONIGHT AT AU PIED DE COCHON AND MET BEAUTIFUL WOMAN NAMED LISA. SEEING HER AGAIN SATURDAY.

—MASON

The solitary yacht, anchored out there alone, surrounded by nothing but miles of the blue Mediterranean, looked small and unimpressive. But it was neither. Eighty meters overall, painted an immaculate white, and fitted throughout with teak and polished brass, its size and splendor drew oohs and aahs even in the marinas of Piraeus where the Onassis fleet docked.

It was midday and the hot sun was beating down from directly overhead. The sea was unusually calm, the anchor line off the yacht's bow almost vertical to the water. High above the water, on the forward deck, a red and white awning rippled gently in what little breeze was blowing. Even under the awning it was oppressively hot. Kopt, wearing only shorts and sandals, could feel the sweat on his hairy back where it rested against the canvas straps of the chaise. Besid him, on a low table, were the remnants of a light lunch. It was his custom on holiday to have a midday nap and he had just closed his eyes when he heard the steward standing over him clearing his throat. He opened his eyes and looked up. "Yes, what is it?"

"I am sorry to disturb you, *Herr* Kopt, but this just arrived." He handed Kopt the telex from Mason.

Kopt sat up and put on his glasses. He read the telex, then turned to the steward. "In my cabin, on the dresser, is a small gold box. Bring it to me." The steward clicked his heels and left. Within minutes, he was back with the box. He handed it to Kopt and waited. Kopt waved him away.

Kopt placed the box on his lap, opened it, and took out a small faded photograph. It was of an old man dressed in the black attire of an Orthodox Jew. Kopt put the photograph to his lips and kissed it. Then he picked up the telex from Mason and showed it to the man in the photograph. "*Zackuth*, my father, *zachuihr It* will not be long now. As we planned, the fly himself is spinning the web for us."

* * *

Viewed from the outside, the *Jeu de Paume* is not impressive, just another gray stone building on the *Place de la Concorde*. But inside, it is a treasure house of Monets, Manets, Cezannes, Lautrecs, Van Go, and other impressionist masterpieces hanging one after another along its walls. Although given over almost entirely to paintings, the museum reserves, on the second floor, a small gallery devoted exclusively to sculpture. It was here Lisa was giving her talk to a group of schoolgirls from *Vitry sur Seine.*

Dressed casually in jeans and a loose cowl-neck sweater, the sleeves pushed up, she was standing next to an easel on which she had put a large photograph of one of Michelangelo's statues. She was pointing to it, explaining why the great Italian sculpture had deliberately left the statue unfinished. She glanced at her watch, saw it was almost noon, and turned to her audience. There, in the middle of it, towering over everyone else, was Mason. All around him the little girls were poking each other, trying to keep from giggling. Lisa put down her pointer and asked if there were any questions. *"Avez-vous des questions a poser?*

The little girls just stood there holding back their giggles. Mason raised his hand. Lisa looked at him and smiled. *"Oui, monsieur?"*

Mason kept his hand in the air. "Would you like to have lunch with me?' He coughed. mean *vouiez-vous* have *le dejeuner* with me?"

The little girls could not contain themselves any longer. They all burst out giggling.

Mason had never tasted the stuff before. He looked across the table at Lisa. "What is this?"

"It is *couscous.* It is something the Algerians brought here to France. In Algeria, they use it as a staple, the way rice and potatos are used in other countries."

"It's good; I like it." He smiled. "You must think I'm nuts. I mean, after the other night at the Pied when I just had whatever you ordered; and now I go and invite you to lunch and ask you to pick the place."

She looked at him. "Well, I am beginning to wonder how you manage when I'm not around."

They both laughed.

The waitress brought a bottle of wine and placed it unceremoniously on the table. Mason filled both their glasses. He picked his up and held it over the table. "Here's to Michelangelo, whatever you were telling your students about him."

Lisa took a sip of her wine. "I was explaining to them that he left the statue unfinished on purpose, to make the point that the figure was really inside the marble, and all he was doing was releasing it.

The actual statue is in Florence." She paused. "I remember the impact it had on me the first time I saw it. I could almost feel the figure inside struggling to get out. It was a strange uncomfortable feeling. I wanted to take a hammer and chisel and—"

"You really know a lot about sculpture. Have you done any writing on the subject?"

She shook her head. "No, it is just a hobby."

"What are you going to write about next? Or is that something I'm not supposed to ask?"

She laughed. "It is all right to ask. I am planning to write two articles. I am going to Wiesbaden next week to do one on Sheik *El dam Kazir* from Abu Dhabi who is going to be there to gamble in the casino."

Mason smiled. "If he is a sheik from Abu Dhabi, he probably has more money than the casino."

"Yes, he is very wealthy. I am told that at a casino on the Riviera, he gave everyone at the table five thousand francs just so they could stay and gamble with him."

"Sounds like an interesting fellow." Mason drank some of his wine. "What's the other article you're going to do; you said there were two."

Lisa refilled their glasses. "On the twenty-seventh of May, I am going to Madrid to do a special piece on Ovilia Maria D'Orteza." She saw that Mason did not recognize the name. "You have not heard of her?"

Mason shook his head. "No."

"She is a woman bullfighter, actually only a young girl. She will be the first female bullfighter ever to fight in the *Plaza de Toros* in Madrid. That is why I am going there."

Mason smiled. "The twenty-seventh, huh? Won't it be pretty hot sitting out there in the sun in late May?"

Lisa reached over and put her hand lightly on Mason's arm. "I won't be sitting in the sun, silly; I will be well back in the shade." She laughed. "Only American tourists sit in the sun."

"Tell me something, Lisa; how did you get into writing anyway?"

She thought for a moment. "I think it was probably because of my father."

Mason almost spilled the spoonful of sugar he was putting in his coffee. "Oh, how so?"

"Well, I can remember when I was a little girl, my father always said to me 'Lisa, when you grow up, you should have a career of your own and be independent; that is very important." She smiled. "I can still hear him saying that to me."

Mason decided to skate over some thin ice. "Are your father and mother still alive?"

Lisa shook her head. "They both died during the war, when I was still an infant. A man, however, who has been like a father to me, is still alive. He's getting old now, though, and is not well. He is—" She caught herself and stopped.

Mason quickly changed the subject. "Speaking of families, would you like to know what my grandfather did for a living?" Lisa was relieved to talk about something else. "Yes."

"He was a bootlegger, a real dishonest-to-goodness one." Lisa frowned. "A bootlegger?"

Mason explained to her what a bootlegger was, telling her all about speakeasies, bathtub gin, and Prohibition generally. "...so, when Prohibition ended, my grandfather suddenly found himself a respectable businessman doing the same thing he would have been sent to jail for."

They both laughed.

Mason ordered more coffee and told Lisa anecdotes about his grandfather, casually mentioning that most of his money had been left to Mason in trust. She seemed at ease, enjoying the stories he was telling her. It was Mason who now felt uncomfortable. He was finding it difficult lying to Lisa.

She smiled at him. "Why do you work at all, Steve? I mean, if you have so much money coming to you?"

Mason turned serious. "Because I don't think I could watch myself shave in the morning if I was just living off someone else's money." He paused. "I suppose that sounds stupid, huh?"

Her eyes met his. "No, Steve, I don't think it sounds stupid at all."

For several minutes, neither of them spoke. They just sat there looking at each other. Mason started to say something, then hesitated. "I was thinking about this fellow—" Lisa waited, her eyes telling him she wanted him to finish what he was going to say. Mason could feel himself blushing a little. "Well, there's this fellow in Frankfurt, a witness in the case I'm working on, that I really should interview. I mean, I have to interview him sometime anyway." He paused. "I could arrange to do it next week and ... well ... I mean ... then maybe I could drop over to Wiesbaden and see this sheik of yours. If you wouldn't mind my being there."

She laughed and touched his arm again. "Why should I mind? I think you might find it interesting. Do you like to gamble?"

"Sometimes. But my real reason would be to see this sheik guy and—" He looked at her. "—and you."

Lisa raised her coffee cup to her lips and took a sip. Her eyes did not leave his. "The name of the place where the sheik will be is the ***Kurhaus*** Casino." She put the cup down and smiled. "And I will be staying at a hotel called the ***Schwatzer Bock.***"

* * *

The first thing Monday morning, Mason went to see Dietz. The Hoch engineer was sitting at his desk having coffee and eating a croissant: "Hi, Steve."

"Hi, Carl, how was your week-end?"

Dietz rested the half-eaten croissant on his cast, held up his hand and made a circle with his fingers. "Great! I went down to the chateau country with Annette."

"Annette, huh? Isn't she the one you were telling me about?

"Yeah, the one who never seems to get enough of it." Dietz smiled. "We were going to visit four or five different chateaus but ended up seeing only the one at Blois. I'm not complaining, you understand; I'd rather spend my time looking at what Annette's got than at any chateau. But the sexy little wench does wear a guy out." He finished his croissant and brushed the crumbs off his cast. "Hey, you want a cup of coffee?"

Mason shook his head. "No, thanks, I'll have one in my office. I've got a lot of reading to do." He paused. "Incidentally, I've changed my mind about our going to see that guy in London this week. I want to see the one in Frankfurt instead. Will you check with him and see if he can meet us on Thursday?"

Dietz was surprised. "Frankfurt? But the guy there isn't even in the top ten on our list. He's just—" He stopped himself and smiled. "Okay, okay, you're the lawyer; I'll call both guys this morning, then have Nadine make the new arrangements."

"Sorry to change plans on you like this."

Dietz shrugged. "Look, like I told you when we started working together on this case, you're the one who calls the shots."

Mason smiled. "Well, my reasons aren't entirely professional. I met this girl who's going to be in Wiesbaden on Thursday and—"

Dietz laughed. "That makes more sense! Now you're beginning to think like I do." He reached in his desk and took out the sales managers file. "The guy in Frankfurt is probably as good as anyone, now that we have Rijksmeer's story in an affidavit." He paused. "I think when you go to Wiesbaden, I'll go over to Heidelberg and see my folks. They're always complaining I never come and visit them." He handed Mason the file. "If you're going to take the girl out to dinner, I know a great restaurant in Wiesbaden; it's called the ***Mutter Engel.*** It's right in the middle of the town."

"The ***Mutter Engel,*** huh? I'll keep it in mind."

Mason took the file and went back to his office.

* * *

The small bar at the *Schwartzer Bock* was crowded but Mason could see that Lisa was not there yet. He found an empty table, waved the waiter away with a sign he was expecting someone, and sat down facing the door. It was only a few minutes later when Lisa arrived. She did not see him at first and stood in the doorway looking around the room. Then she saw him, smiled, and treaded her way through the crowd towards him. He stood up. "Hi." He drew the chair for her to sit down. "Hey, you really look terrific."

She smiled. "Thank you. I'm sorry I was not in when you called the first time."

"No problem. I had to wait for the plane in Frankfurt, so I thought I'd give you a call from there. When I didn't get you, I figured I'd just call again when I got here."

The waiter appeared and Lisa ordered a chardonnay.

"Make it two." Mason laughed. There I go again. "You're right; I don't know how I get along without you." Her eyes met him and she was about to say something; then she changed he mind and looked around the room.

The waiter returned with the two glasses of wine. Mason took his glass and held it up over the little table. "Well, here's to old Sheik-el-whats-his-face, who is going to be interviewed tonight by the most beautiful woman in the world."

Lisa smiled at the compliment. "Actually it is not the sheik I will be interviewing; it will be his confidant."

Mason put his glass down and looked at her. "What were you going to say a minute ago?" She lowered her eyes and shook her head. He pleaded with her. "Come on, tell me." She looked up at him, blushing slightly, something he had not seen her do before. "I was going to ask you if you would like to have dinner tonight." She paused. "Of course, if you have other plans—"

"I don't." Mason reached across the table and took her hand in his. "If I did, I'd break them." For a moment, neither of them said anything Then Mason leaned back and smiled. "Besides, how would I know what to order if you weren't there with me??

Lisa laughed. "My interview should not take long, but I would like to watch the sheik gamble a bit. Do you mind having a late dinner, around nine-thirty?"

"That's fine. I suppose we should make a reservation."

She put her hand on his arm. "I will do that. I want to take you to a restaurant I know, the *Mutter Engel;* it is—"

Mason threw his head back and laughed. "The *Mutter Engel!*"

Lisa looked at him, puzzled. "Yes, why are you laughing?"

Mason reached in his pocket, took out a slip of paper, and handed it to her. On it was written the name *Mutter Engel.* He smiled. "Carl Dietz, the fellow I'm working with on the Hoch case, told me it was the best restaurant in Wiesbaden. I wrote the name down because..." He looked at her. "...because that's where I was going to ask you to have dinner with me tonight."

* * *

The croupiers at the *Kurhaus* Casino reminded Mason of characters in an old horror movie he had seen called The Living Dead. Wearing tightly tailored tuxedos and strategically positioned around the room, their small beady eyes caught the slightest movement of a chip anywhere on the green felt tables. Their faces were all the same cold expressionless masks of total disinterest, a marked contrast to the color and excitement of the casino.

Everywhere Mason looked were blackjack, faro, craps, and baccarat tables, each one surrounded by its small group of devotees. The main action, however, was in the center of the room where most of the gamblers were crowded around a large roulette table. Sitting at the table, close to the giant wheel, was the Sheik el elam Kazir. Behind him, hovering like a flock of predatory birds, was his retinue: a dozen fierce-looking Arabs in flowing *galabiyahs* and headpieces held by twisted cord *'igals.*

As Mason entered with Lisa, one of the Arabs, wearing a gold *'igal,* leaned over and whispered in the Sheik's ear. The Sheik nodded. The Arab with the gold *'igal* left the table to meet with Lisa for the interview he had promised.

Mason saw the Sheik's confidant approaching them. He left Lisa to deal with him, and walked over to the cashier's cage. He handed the teller two thousand francs. The teller pointed to the different colored chips in the racks beside him. "Welche farbe wollen sie?"

Mason smiled. "Sorry, I don't speak German. Do you speak English?"

The teller did not smile back. "Of course. What color chips do you want? The white ones are fifty *Deutschemarks;* the reds are one hundred; the blues are five hundred."

Mason wondered if he could get the guy to crack a smile by asking for five hundred worth of *Deutschemarks* in blue chip. He looked at the guy's face and decided he would never get the joke. "Give me three reds and the rest whites." As quickly as Mason had asked for them, the chips appeared in front of him, spread out in neatly countable rows. He scooped them into his pocket, walked over to the roulette table, and squeezed in beside a woman gambler.

The Sheik had just won and was adding his winnings to the pile of blue chips in front of him. Mason stood for a moment watching the action at the table. Each time the wheel was spun, the Sheik placed a bet and his entire retinue leaned forward to watch with him as the little ball, at first just a blur whirling around the circumference of the wheel, lost its centrifugal force and bounced down capriciously over the numbers, fmally settling into the pocket of the one it had chosen the winner. When it chose the Sheik's number, the Arabs behind him all elbowed each other and grunted approval. When it did not, which was more often, they growled and cursed and muttered until the ball was thrown onto the wheel again.

Mason leaned over the table and put five of his white chips on number twenty-three. He felt his arm bump against the woman beside him. "Excuse me."

The woman turned around. She was holding an empty highball glass and a cigarette in one hand and a handful of red chips in the other. Fortyish and although not bad looking, she was too heavily made up in an attempt to appear younger. She was also slightly drunk. She looked up and Mason and smiled. "It is quite all right." She twisted her body sideways to make more room for him at the table. "Here, move in a little so you can reach easier." As Mason stepped closer to the table, he felt her body press against him.

"DREISSEG-EIN!" The little ball had chosen number thirty-one. The croupier's rake swept Mason's chips off to the side. The Sheik had not won either. The woman moved closer to Mason, her breasts pressing against his arm. She smiled. "You are an

American?"

Mason put another five chips on number twenty-three. "Yes." "My name is Helmie. I am from Munich. I am not having very good luck. Are you?"

Mason just shrugged and watched as the wheel slowed down again.

"ZWANZIG-DREI!" The little ball dropped into number twenty-three. Mason smiled as the croupier's rake pushed a pile of chips over to him. The woman slipped her arm around his and laughed. "You won! I

have brought you good luck!" She held up her empty glass. "Perhaps you will get me a drink."

Mason had one of the attendants bring her a drink, tipped him, and then started to leave.

"Oh, you're not leaving?" She tightened her grip on his arm and pressed her pelvis against him. "Stay and play some more; your luck is just beginning."

Mason looked across the room to where Lisa was standing talking to the Sheik's confidant. He wanted to signal her that he was doing his best to extricate himself from the woman who was now all over him. Lisa had her back to him and he could not get her attention. Gently but firmly, he pried the woman's arm from around his. "Thanks, but I think I'll try a little blackjack." He smiled politely. "But I'll leave all my roulette luck here with you." He pushed his way back out of the crowd at the table.

The woman followed him. "I'll come with you and bring you luck at blackjack too." She locked her arm around his again.

Mason saw he was not getting rid of her. "Okay, but first I have to go to the men's room. You go ahead and warm up the game for me." He broke away from her and headed for the lobby of the casino. When he got there, he looked back over his shoulder. She was still standing where he had left her. He stood for a moment in the middle of the lobby trying to decide what to do. Maybe if I stay out here for a while, she'll attach herself so someone else, he thought. He glanced at his watch. It was not quite nine yet. He looked into the casino again. She was still standing there watching him. She waved and started towards him. It's no good, he decided; she's coming after me. He stepped around the corner of the lobby so he was out of her sight, then slipped out the front door of the *Kurhaus.*

Back in the casino, the Sheik's confidant repeated his answer to Lisa's question. She turned to him, blushing slightly. "I am sorry, I did not hear what you said. I was distracted by something for a moment."

In the gardens outside the *Kurhaus* it was now dark. Night had crept in behind the stately old linden trees and the little lamps in the flower beds had been turned on. Mason hurried down one of the paths until he came to the large iron gate leading out to the *Wilhelmstrasse.* He stopped and looked back. The woman had not come out after him. He decided to wait a few more minutes before going back in. He glanced out through the gate. Parked only a few yards away was the black Mercedes with registration DX751P. The front seat was empty. The side windows were heavily tinted and he could not tell whether anyone was in the back seat. He heard footsteps behind him.

Someone was coming across the gardens. He slipped into the shadow of the gate. A figure suddenly appeared out of the darkness. It was not the woman from the casino; it was a man wearing a tuxedo. Mason's eyes narrowed. He stepped back deeper in the shadow as

Gray Vest hurried past without seeing him, went through the gate and up the street to the Mercedes. The back window of the car rolled down a few inches and Gray Vest bent down and spoke into it.

Mason bit his lip. It was time for an accounting, he decided. This guy had been following him long enough; it was time to confront the bastard and fmd out what the hell his game was. He walked out through the gate and started towards the Mercedes. Gray Vest saw him coming and snarled something into the window of the car. The window rolled up quickly. As Mason reached the Mercedes, Gray Vest stepped in front of him and blocked his way. Mason stopped. "What the hell are you following me for?"

Gray Vest just stood there. *"Ich spreche niche englisch."* "Look, fella, I know you've been following me. What the hell do you want?"

Gray Vest continued to block Mason's way. *"Ich spreche niche englisch."*

"Okay, fella, have it your way." Mason pushed past him and reached for the handle of the door to the Mercedes. "Maybe your friend in here understands English. I ask him what this is all about."

The blow was perfectly placed, hard and delivered with a quickness he never expected from a man as big as Gray Vest. It caught Mason on the back of the neck, just below the hairline. It dropped him like a stone. He was out like a light before he hit the sidewalk.

* * *

Mason woke up disoriented. He could tell it was morning; the bright sunlight was streaming in through the window. He could feel himself lying on a bed, still fully dressed. He started to lift himself up on his elbows and felt a sharp pain stab at the back of his head. He lowered himself gingerly back down. He looked around as much as he could without moving. He was in a hotel somewhere—but where? He reached behind his head and felt his neck. It was sore to the touch. And there was something else: a strange taste in his mouth—no, not a taste, a smell, a strong pungent smell. He saw a telephone beside the bed. He reached over slowly, picked it up, and dragged it back onto the pillow, next to his head. A heavy German voice came out of the receiver. *"Hallo? Hallo?"*

Mason moved the telephone down to his mouth. "Where am

I?"

"Hallo?"

Mason tried again. "What's the name of this place?" The voiced spoke English. "What can I do for you?" "This place; what's the name of it?

"It is the *Zwn Ritter.*"

"Am I in Wiesbaden?"

"Yes, of course. Is something wrong?"

"No, everything is all right. Thanks "

Mason hung up. The ***Zum Ritter?*** He did not remember that name on the list of hotels Dietz gave him in Paris. He looked up at the ornate ceiling. How the hell did I get here? The last thing I remember is reaching for the door handle of the Mercedes and—He had to smile to himself. Whoever that guy Gray Vest is, the bastard sure knows how to put someone out of action quick. I wonder who the hell it was in the back seat of the Mercedes I wasn't suppose to see? He continued to stare at the. ceiling Well, one thing is clear now; I haven't got everyone over here fooled; someone knows I'm not here just to get affidavits in the Hoch case. He frowned. But they couldn't possibly know the real reason I'm here is to—Suddenly he remembered—Holy Jesus! Lisa! He bolted upright—but too quickly. The pain, waiting at the back of his neck, stabbed into his head like a hot knife He had to grab the bedpost and hold on until the pain subsided. Then slowly he was able to get up and struggle into the bathroom. He knelt down beside the tub, put his head under the faucet, and turned on the cold water.

While he let the cold water run down the back of his neck, he took stock. The first problem was not Gray Vest and his friend in the nd felt a sharp pain stab at the back of his head. He lowered himself gingerly back down. He looked around as much as he could without moving. He was in a hotel somewhere—but where? He reached behind his head and felt his neck. It was sore to the touch. And there was something else: a strange taste in his mouth—no, not a taste, a smell, a strong pungent smell. He saw a telephone beside the bed. He reached over slowly, picked it up, and dragged it back onto the pillow, next to his head. A heavy German voice came out of the receiver. *"Hallo? Hallo?"*

Mason moved the telephone down to his mouth. "Where am *I?"*

"Hallo?"

Mason tried again. "What's the name of this place?" The voiced spoke English. "What can I do for you?" "This place; what's the name of it?

"It is the *Zwn Ritter."*

"Am I in Wiesbaden?"

"Yes, of course. Is something wrong?"

"No, everything is all right. Thanks "

Mason hung up. The ***Zum Ritter?*** He did not remember that name on the list of hotels Dietz gave him in Paris. He looked up at the ornate ceiling. How the hell did I get here? The last thing I remember is reaching for the door handle of the Mercedes and—He had to smile to himself. Whoever that guy Gray Vest is, the bastard sure knows how to put someone out of action quick. I wonder who the hell it was in the back seat of the Mercedes I wasn't suppose to see? He continued to stare at the. ceiling Well, one thing is clear now; I haven't got everyone over here fooled; someone knows I'm not here just to get affidavits in the Hoch case. He frowned. But they couldn't possibly know the real reason I'm here is to—Suddenly he remembered—Holy Jesus! Lisa! He bolted upright—but too quickly. The pain, waiting at the back of his neck, stabbed into his head like a hot knife He had to grab the bedpost and hold on until the pain subsided. Then slowly he was able to get up and struggle into the bathroom. He knelt down beside the tub, put his head under the faucet, and turned on the cold water.

While he let the cold water run down the back of his neck, he took stock. The first problem was not Gray Vest and his friend in the

The Sheik had just won and was adding his winnings to the pile of blue chips in front of him. Mason stood for a moment watching the action at the table. Each time the wheel was spun, the Sheik placed a bet and his entire retinue leaned forward to watch with him as the little ball, at first just a blur whirling around the circumference of the wheel, lost its centrifugal force and bounced down capriciously over the numbers, fmally settling into the pocket of the one it had chosen the winner. When it chose the Sheik's number, the Arabs behind him all elbowed each other and grunted approval. When it did not, which was more often, they growled and cursed and muttered until the ball was thrown onto the wheel again.

Mason leaned over the table and put five of his white chips on number twenty-three. He felt his arm bump against the woman beside him. "Excuse me."

The woman turned around. She was holding an empty highball glass and a cigarette in one hand and a handful of red chips in the other. Fortyish and although not bad looking, she was too heavily made up in an attempt to appear younger. She was also slightly drunk. She looked up and Mason and smiled. "It is quite all right." She twisted her body sideways to make more room for him at the table. "Here, move in a little so you can reach easier." As Mason stepped closer to the table, he felt her body press against him.

"DREISSEG-EIN!" The little ball had chosen number thirty-one. The croupier's rake swept Mason's chips off to the side. The Sheik had not won either. The woman moved closer to Mason, her breasts pressing against his arm. She smiled. "You are an

American?"

Mason put another five chips on number twenty-three. "Yes." "My name is Helmie. I am from Munich. I am not having very good luck. Are you?"

Mason just shrugged and watched as the wheel slowed down again.

"ZWANZIG-DREI!" The little ball dropped into number twenty-three. Mason smiled as the croupier's rake pushed a pile of chips over to him. The woman slipped her arm around his and laughed. "You won! I

have brought you good luck!" She held up her empty glass. "Perhaps you will get me a drink."

Mason had one of the attendants bring her a drink, tipped him, and then started to leave.

"Oh, you're not leaving?" She tightened her grip on his arm and pressed her pelvis against him. "Stay and play some more; your luck is just beginning."

Mason looked across the room to where Lisa was standing talking to the Sheik's confidant. He wanted to signal her that he was doing his best to extricate himself from the woman who was now all over him. Lisa had her back to him and he could not get her attention. Gently but firmly, he pried the woman's arm from around his. "Thanks, but I think I'll try a little blackjack." He smiled politely. "But I'll leave all my roulette luck here with you." He pushed his way back out of the crowd at the table.

The woman followed him. "I'll come with you and bring you luck at blackjack too." She locked her arm around his again.

Mason saw he was not getting rid of her. "Okay, but first I have to go to the men's room. You go ahead and warm up the game for me." He broke away from her and headed for the lobby of the casino. When he got there, he looked back over his shoulder. She was still standing where he had left her. He stood for a moment in the middle of the lobby trying to decide what to do. Maybe if I stay out here for a while, she'll attach herself so someone else, he thought. He glanced at his watch. It was not quite nine yet. He looked into the casino again. She was still standing there watching him. She waved and started towards him. It's no good, he decided; she's coming after me. He stepped around the corner of the lobby so he was out of her sight, then slipped out the front door of the *Kurhaus.*

Back in the casino, the Sheik's confidant repeated his answer to Lisa's question. She turned to him, blushing slightly. "I am sorry, I did not hear what you said. I was distracted by something for a moment."

In the gardens outside the *Kurhaus* it was now dark. Night had crept in behind the stately old linden trees and the little lamps in the flower beds had been turned on. Mason hurried down one of the paths until he came to the large iron gate leading out to the *Wilhelmstrasse.* He stopped and

looked back. The woman had not come out after him. He de
a few more minutes before going back in. He glanced out
gate. Parked only a few yards away was the black Me
registration DX751P. The front seat was empty. The side wi
heavily tinted and he could not tell whether anyone was in th
He heard footsteps behind him.

Someone was coming across the gardens. He slipped into
of the gate. A figure suddenly appeared out of the darkness. It
woman from the casino; it was a man wearing a tuxedo. M
narrowed. He stepped back deeper in the shadow as

Gray Vest hurried past without seeing him, went through t
up the street to the Mercedes. The back window of the car ro
few inches and Gray Vest bent down and spoke into it.

Mason bit his lip. It was time for an accounting, he decide
had been following him long enough; it was time to confront
and fmd out what the hell his game was. He walked out throu
and started towards the Mercedes. Gray Vest saw him coming a
something into the window of the car. The window rolled up
Mason reached the Mercedes, Gray Vest stepped in front o
blocked his way. Mason stopped. "What the hell are you foll
for?"

Gray Vest just stood there. *"Ich spreche niche englisch."* "Lo
know you've been following me. What the hell do you want?"

Gray Vest continued to block Mason's way. *"Ich spreche nich*

"Okay, fella, have it your way." Mason pushed past him an
for the handle of the door to the Mercedes. "Maybe your frie
understands English. I ask him what this is all about."

The blow was perfectly placed, hard and delivered with a qui
never expected from a man as big as Gray Vest. It caught Mas
back of the neck, just below the hairline. It dropped him like a s
was out like a light before he hit the sidewalk.

* * *

Mason woke up disoriented. He could tell it was morning; t
sunlight was streaming in through the window. He could fee
lying on a bed, still fully dressed. He started to lift himself up on hi

Mercedes; he'd deal with them later. And next time, he'd be more careful; he'd keep his eyes on the bastard's hands, that's for sure. Right now, there was something more important to worry about: Lisa. He had to get in touch with her right away and explain what happened. He turned off the water, stood up and looked in the mirror. His eyes were bloodshot and he needed a shave, but he felt better. He went back into the bedroom and picked up the telephone. Again, the heavy German voice answered. *"Hallo?"*

"I want to call the *Schwartzer Bock.*"

"The *Schwartzer Bock?* Certainly. Please hang up. I will ring you when you are connected." Mason hung up and waited. A moment later the telephone rang again. It was a different German voice this time. *"Hallo? Schwartzer Bock."*

"I want to be connected to the room of Miss Lisa Helms "

There was a pause, then the voice again. "I am sorry, *Frauline* Helms has checked out."

"I'm Mr. Mason. Did she leave any message for me?"

There was another pause. "No, there is no message for you."

Mason jiggled the receiver until he got the desk at the ***Zum Ritter*** again. "I want you to make another call for me, to the Hotel ***Baren."***

"Certainly. Hang up please."

When the telephone rang again, it was the desk at the hotel where Mason was staying. "Hotel ***Baren."***

"This is Mr. Mason. Are there any messages for me?" "No, ***Herr*** Mason, there are no messages."

Mason hung up and thought for a moment. He picked his jacket up off the bed and patted it down. His wallet and passport were still there. He went through the pockets. Nothing had been taken. Even the red chips he had won at the casino were in one of them. He looked at his watch. It was a little after ten. He put on is jacket, left the room, and took the elevator down to the lobby.

The concierge listened to him, and then shrugged his shoulders. "I do not know who he was, sir; I can only tell you he was a very large man and was wearing a tuxedo."

"Did he say anything?"

The concierge shook his head. "Only that you had had too much to drink, and that he wanted to put you in one of our rooms for the night."

"Anything else?"

"He said something about your being an American businessman and not accustomed to our strong German beer. He gave me your name and paid your bill in advance."

"Was he alone?"

The concierge nodded. "Yes, although—" He smiled. "If I may say so, sir, although your friend is a very large man, he needed the help of one of our porters to carry you to your room." He paused. "Is there anything else I can do for you?"

Mason thought for a moment. "You can tell me how to get to the *Mutter Engel.*"

The concierge looked at his watch. "You know, of course, it will not be open at this hour."

"Just tell me the quickest way to get there."

"It is best for you go by taxi. I will summon one for you." He rang a little bell on the desk and barked a command in German to one of the porters. Then he turned to Mason again. "If you will go outside now, your taxi should be here in a minute or two."

Mason was out of the taxi almost before it had stopped in front of the ***Mutter Engel.*** Inside, the place was empty except for a solitary waiter refilling the salt and pepper shakers on the tables. Mason caught his attention. "Do you speak English?"

The waiter shook his head and pointed to the back of the restaurant where another man was standing, making notes on a large menu. As Mason approached him, he tucked the menu under his arm. "What can I do for you?"

"I need to talk to someone who was here last night. Were you here then?"

The man nodded. "Of course. I am the maitre d'; I am here every evening the restaurant is open. What do you wish to know?"

"Last night, was there a woman here, a tall woman with blond hair and—"

The maitre d' interrupted him. "Yes, she was here; I remember her. She came alone and—" He stopped. He looked at Mason, waiting. Mason reached into his pocket, took out one of the red chips from the casino, and placed it on the table. "And what?"

The maitre d' smiled and continued. "She came here at nine-. thirty. When I asked to take her order, she said she was waiting for someone." He picked up the red chip and slipped it into his vest pocket. "She waited for almost an hour, and had several glasses of wine. Then at about half past ten, she paid her bill, and left without having dinner.

* * *

The telephone on Mason's desk rang. He grabbed it while it was still ringing. "Hello, Andre, did you find out—" His voice dropped. "Oh, it's you."

The voice on the other end was Deschamps. He laughed. "You sound disappointed, Steve."

Mason apologized. "Sorry, Lloyd. I didn't mean to sound that way. It's just that I was expecting a call from Doucette. What can I do for you?"

"I've just finished talking with Alex in Boston. He wants you to give him a call as soon as you can. He'll be in his office for another hour; then he has to go to a meeting."

"I'll put a call into him right away. Thanks."

Mason hung up and was about to buzz for Nadine when Dietz burst in waving the transcript of their interview with Hoch's sales manager in London. "Hey, Steve, this is great! I just got it from the stenographer we used in London last week. Our sales manager there really gave us some good stuff about what Chimique's been doing in the U.K." He flipped through the typewritten pages. "Listen to this. 'In 1969, three of our sales engineers in the Glasgow Office left the company to go to work for Chimique.'" Dietz slapped the transcript against his cast. "1969! Steve, that was more than a year before Chimique came out with its process! And here, look, it says all three were engineers who had worked on the development of Hoch's process and had signed secrecy agreements." He handed the transcript to Mason. "Well, you're the lawyer, but is that a smoking gun or what?"

Mason smiled at Dietz's enthusiasm. "It's pretty good, Carl." "Now all we have to do is go and take the depositions of these three guys and find out what—"

Mason shook his head. "I'm afraid it's not as simple as that." .Dietz frowned. "Why not?"

"Well, until there's an actual lawsuit pending, we can't make them answer any questions if they don't want to. If we tried to take their depositions now, they'd just tell us to go to hell. Even after we bring the lawsuit, we may have trouble getting them to answer any questions before the actual trial. Remember, we're dealing with French and English law" He pointed to the transcript. "But if you're finished with that, leave it with me. I'd like to read it before I talk to our French lawyers."

As soon as Dietz left, Mason buzzed for Nadine.

"Oui, monsieur?"

"Nadine, I want you to put a call in to Mr. Templeton in the Boston Office. He's expecting to hear from me."

The little secretary smiled and left, closing the door behind her. Mason slid the transcript to one side and moved the telephone in front of him. Then he sat back and waited. He took himself to task. Well, Mason, you've done it; you've gone and screwed it all up. It's been three months since Wiesbaden and you still can't fmd Lisa. What a dumb play not to fmd out where she lives. Somewhere on the Left Bank, that's all you know. Big help! That's like knowing she lives in Boston, somewhere in Back Bay. He shook his head. Everything he had tried had drawn a blank. She had not been back to the Pied since the night they were there together. Francois promised to let him know if she made a reservation, but chances were she was deliberately staying away from the place. He had checked the telephone directory, even called the *Jue de Palme* and the Swedish Embassy: all blanks. He thought back to the casino and swore under his breath. That was it; that was where I blew it, he told himself. I let that crazy woman hang all over me at the roulette table, even go and get her a drink.

Then I go out to the lobby, she follows me, and it looks like we've got something going. Then, to cap it off, I don't show at the *Mutter Engel* where Lisa is waiting for me. No wonder she's ticked! He shook his head.

Well, my only hope now is Doucette. He managed a smile Good old Andre, 'If she is anywhere in Paris, *monsieur, I* will find her for you,' he said. But so far, even Doucette, with all his contacts, had not come up with anything.

The telephone rang. It was the switchboard operator. "Mr. Mason?"

"Yes."

"I have Mr. Templeton on the line."

"Fine. Put him through."

Templeton's voice came on the other end. "Hello, Steve?" "Yes, I'm here."

"How are things going over there? I hope you're not letting work prevent you from getting around to see a few of the sights."

"No, I'm getting to see quite a lot. How is everything in the office? Any problems with any of the cases I left behind?"

"No, everything is under control." There was a pause. "Steve, the reason I asked you to call me is...well, I'd like to know what your impression is of your assignment over there.?'

"My impression?"

"Yes. I don't want you to tell me anything about what you're doing; we've got an agreement with the client on that. But if you can, I'd like you to give me your impression in general."

Mason thought for a moment. "Well, it's an unusual assignment; I mean it's not your basic trial lawyer's kind of thing But so far, it seems legitimate enough. Why? Is there something wrong at that end?"

"No, it's just that...well, you remember my saying I thought this fellow, Kopt, was rather an odd duck?"

Mason smiled to himself. "Yes, I do. What has he done now?"

There was a pause. "Nothing But that's it. I mean we haven't heard word one from him since the day he met with you at the Ritz. His retainer check arrived the day after you left, from the Chase Manhattan Bank in New York. But no one in the office has had any communication at all with Kopt himself. Normally, I wouldn't be concerned but—" Templeton paused. "But when you've been practicing law as long as I have, Steve, you develop a sort of sixth sense about clients. And I have the sense there's something fishy about this fellow, Kopt. I can't put my finger on it but I feel it in my bones. It may be just my imagination but…in any event, that's why I wanted to hear what your impression was at that end."

Mason was tempted to tell Templeton about Gray Vest and the incident in Wiesbaden, but decided against it. "Well, as I said, the assignment is a little out of the ordinary. But I'm not being asked to do anything illegal or unethical, and that's what we agreed. So, I'm prepared to stick with it until we know of some reason I shouldn't."

"Okay, Steve, as long as things seem all right at your end, I guess we should go along with Kopt, at least for the time being." There was a pause. "But, Steve—"

"Yes?"

"If anything happens, anything at all, that raises any question in your mind, I want you to get in touch with me right away. Will you do that?"

"All right."

"Well, that's all I wanted to talk to you about. I'm glad you're finding time to get around a bit over there."

"Thanks."

"Good-bye, Steve." "Good-bye."

As Mason hung up, Doucette appeared at the door. Mason motioned for him to come in. "Any news, Andre?"

Doucette waddled over and stood in front on Mason's desk. "I am afraid, *monsieur*, that as you say in America, I have the good news and the bad news."

"I'll take the good news first."

Doucette sat down. "I have found where your *Mademoiselle* Helms lives."

Mason jumped up. "Great! I knew I could count on you,

Andre! Where does she live?"

"At number *15 Rue Charles V*. It is in the *Marais* section, near the *Place de Vosges*. She has a small apartment on the second floor and lives there alone. She has been living there since—"

"What's the bad news?"

"She is not there."

"What do you mean, she is not there?"

"She has left Paris."

"Do we know where she has gone?"

"No."

"How long is she going to be away; do we know that?" "No, the concierge said—"

"You had someone speak to the concierge?"

Doucette managed a smile. "I spoke with the concierge myself, *monsieur;* she is the wife of the brother of a very good friend of mine, and I—"

"What did she say?"

"Only that *Mademoiselle* Helms said she would be away for some time."

Mason pounded his fist on the desk. "Damn! So we don't know where the hell she is, or when the hell she's corning back!"

Doucette's chin dropped down on his wrinkled shirt. "I am afraid that is the case, *monsieur. I* am sorry I have failed you."

Mason walked around from behind his desk and put his hand on Doucette's shoulder. "You haven't failed me, Andre; you did a hell of a job just fmding out where she lives. In a city as big as Paris, I don't know how you—"

Doucette stood up, shaking his head. "Yes, but now she has left the city, I cannot be of much help to you, **monsieur.** In Paris, I have certain connections, yes. But outside the city, I am afraid—"

"It's okay. At least we know where she lives. She's got to come back sometime."

Doucette's eyes brightened a little. **"Oui, monsieur.** And when she does, I will be notified right away. I have made arrangements for that. And you will know as soon as I know; I promise you."

After Doucette left, Mason sat at his desk for several minutes thinking There had to be something he could do besides sit around waiting for Lisa to come back. She might be gone for weeks, even months. If he only knew where she went, or—He suddenly remembered something. He leaped from his chair and rushed out of his office. "Nadine!"

"Oui, **monsieur?"**

"Nadine, I want you to do something for me right away. Get me a ticket on the next flight to Madrid. Call one of the hotels there and get me a room." He paused. "And pick a hotel that's near the big bullring, the ***Plaza de Toros.***

* * *

In the *Plaza de Toros* the crowd was gathering. The ticket windows of the massive coliseum had opened and the long lines extending out into the spacious open square were shuffling towards them. The square, blazing with the hot afternoon sun of central Spain, bustled with excitement. *Madrilenos* were pouring in from all directions, peddlers of programs and souvenirs were hawking their wares in strident voices, and people were strumming guitars and singing, all adding to the cacophony. On the nearby *calles,* the *aficionados* at the little café tables were finishing their *tapas* and Sherries and signaling for their bills.

Mason looked at the long lines at the ticket windows and was glad he had bought his at the hotel. For several minutes, he stood in the center of the plaza hoping to spot Lisa somewhere in the crowd. Then he shook his head. It was pointless trying to find her out there where so many people were milling around and new ones coming all the time Inside the arena, where everyone would be sitting down; that's where he'd have the best chance, he decided. He waited a few more minutes, then headed for the arena. He followed the crowd toward the large entrance, of both sides of which the walls were covered with colorful posters of matadors performing *veronicas* and *estocadas,* their slender bodies arched gracefully over the sharp horns of huge Andalusian bulls. These were the matadors who would fight in the *Plaza de Toros* today. Mason saw that one of the posters was of Ovilia Maria D' Orteza, the young woman bullfighter Lisa had told him about in the Algerian restaurant in Paris.

Mason had read all about Ovilia Maria in a magazine on the plane yesterday. She was the first woman ever to be promoted to *Matadora de Toros* and invited to fight in the huge bullring in Madrid. Her father was one of Spain's most popular matadors until he was badly gored in a *corrida* in Seville. According to the magazine, Ovilia Maria was sixteen when she killed her first bull. It was in a *corrida* for beginners in Linares. She was so good the crowd demanded she be awarded an ear. After Linares, and while still a *novillera,* she fought in dozens of small towns throughout Andalusia, showing remarkable poise and bravery. Even the most skeptical *aficionados,* after watching her, agreed she was as fearless as any man. Now barely nineteen, she would have a chance to display her courage and skill in the most prestigious bullring in all Spain. One Madrid newspaper suggested she be permitted to fight smaller bulls.

Ovilia Maria was indignant, insisting her bulls be animals weighing over four hundred kilos and every bit as dangerous as the other matadors would face.

Mason glanced at his watch. It was a few minutes before four-thirty. He took a last look around, and then joined the flow of people streaming into the coliseum. The attendant at the gate took his ticket and motioned him to an opening marked ***SOMBRE.*** He walked through the opening, turned, and looked up. The stands already were almost filled. He glanced down at the bullring. The *toreros* in their tight colorful suits of lights were practicing with their *caleas* and joking nervously with each other. Mason spotted Ovilia Maria, noticeably smaller than the rest, her light, peaches and cream, skin a marked contrast to the long black hair falling from under her *montera.*

Mason walked slowly along the aisle at the foot of the stands, squinting up into the sea of faces above, trying to shield his eyes from the late afternoon sun pouring in over the top of the coliseum. He did not see Lisa in the first two sections. He continued past the third She was not there either. He frowned. Maybe she—

A trumpet sounded.

High up in the stands, at the top of the center section, a silver-haired man, wearing a black suit and dark sun glasses rose in his box seat and nodded to the crowd. Beside him were several soldiers of the ***Civilia Guardia,*** rifles slung over their shoulders. He stood up, took off his sun glasses and looked out over the arena. He stood there for several moments, then took out a white handkerchief and draped it over the front of his box. The trumpet sounded again The man was the ***Presidente de la Corrida*** and had just given the signal for the bullfights to begin

Mason was still making his way along the aisle, looking for Lisa. He did not see her in the large center section, and moved to the next one.

Out in the bullring, the parade of ***toreros*** was beginning. Leading it were the two mounted ***Alqualiles in*** their traditional seventeenth century costumes. Behind them, marching in two columns, were the matadors, followed by the paunchy ***banderillos*** and the unpopular but essential ***picadors.*** Bringing up the rear of the parade was the stark reminder of the ***corrida's*** grim ingredient: the mule-drawn harness and chain that would drag the dead bull's carcass from the arena.

Mason was at the last section and still no Lisa. Maybe she's not here after all, he thought. Maybe she changed her mind and decided to write an article on something else. Or maybe she just—He turned and started back along the aisle to check all the sections again. Maybe she came in afterwards, or maybe he just missed her the first time. He was walking slower now, looking up harder and longer into the faces in the stands. The blazing sun was stinging his eyes, making them water. He kept going, kept looking, kept telling himself: She's got to be here! I've got to find her!

The trumpet sounded again. The crowd fell silent. Everyone's eyes were fixed on a heavy wooden gate at the far side of the ring. For several moments nothing happened, everyone just watching and waiting. Suddenly the wooden gate burst open and a huge black bull, his massive head lowered, charged out into the empty ring. Then, abruptly, it stopped and stood still, looking puzzled. It raised its head and rotated it slowly from side to side, surveying the large open space around it. Something caught its eye, something moving on the other side of the ring. *A peone* from the first matador's *cuadilla* had just stepped out a few feet from the *barrera* and was attracting the bull's attention with a red cloak. The bull lowered his head and charged.

The ***peone*** fled back to the ***barrera,*** slipping behind the wooden ***burladero*** just in time. The bull butted furiously at the narrow opening in the ***burladero,*** trying to reach the ***peone*** with its deadly horns. The crowd screamed with delight. Only a few feet from his ***peone,*** standing behind the ***barrera,*** was the first matador of the ***corrida,*** waiting to enter the ring. He had been watching the bull carefully, measuring the speed with which it charged his ***peone.*** Now, he would have to use the ***capea*** to test the animal's intelligence and ability to change direction quickly. He stood, nervously adjusting and readjusting his ***montera,*** waiting.

The trumpet sounded.

The matador folded the large magenta and gold ***capea*** over his arm and stepped out from behind the ***barrera.*** He paused for a moment and made the sign of the cross on his chest. Then, taking a deep breath, he strutted out into the bright sunlight toward the bull. The crowd rose to its feet, cheering. Everyone's eyes were riveted on the drama below—everyone's except Mason's. Mason was oblivious to what was happening in the ring. For now, high up in the stands, only a few rows from the ***Presidente's*** box, he saw Lisa!

Out in the ring, the matador, holding the *capea* in front of him, inched closer to the bull. Lisa, like everyone around her, was watching, waiting for the bull to charge. She did not see Mason rushing up the cement steps towards her. It was not until he had climbed over a dozen protesting Spaniards and squeezed down beside her that she saw him. She looked up in surprise. "Steve! What are you doing here?"

"Looking for you. I've been looking everywhere."

She flushed slightly. "Oh?"

"Yes, I looked all over Paris for you. I even checked at the place where you live."

She frowned. "How did you find out where I lived?"

"I found out." He caught his breath. "The woman there said you had left Paris. She said she didn't know when you'd be back." He paused. "I didn't know what the hell to do. Then I remembered your telling me you were coming here on the twenty-seventh."

Lisa did not look at him. "Well, you have come a long way. I hope you enjoy the bullfights. Ovilia Maria, the woman matador I told you about is going to fight next. I interviewed her this morning and—"

Mason interrupted her. "Listen, Lisa, I want to explain what happened in Wiesbaden."

She continued to look straight ahead. "You do not have to explain. I am not really interested in what you did in Wiesbaden. That is your business, not mine." She paused. "If you wanted to go off and spend your evening with someone else, that was up to you. But I had planned to have dinner with you and...forget it. It is just that there were other things I could have arranged to do in Wiesbaden too, you know."

Down in the ring, the matador was standing only a few feet from the bull, taunting it with the *capea.* The bull lowered its head and charged. The matador stepped to one side and drew the animal past him into the heavy cloth of the *capea.* The bull turned and charged again. The matador, his feet planted firmly in the hot sand, swept the *capea* over the bull's horns in a classic *veronica.* The crowd applauded. Lisa applauded with them.

Mason grabbed her arm, and made her look at him. "Will you listen to me for a minute. It's important to me that you know what really happened in Wiesbaden. If you want to be mad at me, or not interested in me, okay; but not until you've at least given me a chance to tell you what really happened." He continued to hold her arm firmly.

"All right, I'll listen."

Mason let go of her arm. "I left the casino that night to get away from that crazy woman who was hanging all over me. The number I played won and she insisted I get her a drink for bringing me luck. As soon as I got the drink for her, I left the table. But she came after me. I decided the only way to get rid of her was to go outside and wait until it was time to meet you. I went out and walked around in the gardens. Then I spotted this guy with a gray vest who's been following me since I came over here and..." Mason told her the whole story of what had happened when he tried to see who was in the back of the Mercedes. "...Whoever it was in the Mercedes, Gray Vest sure didn't want me to see him. I know it was dumb of me to turn my back on him; I should never have done that. Anyway, the next thing I knew, it was the following morning and I was in some hotel called the *Zum Ritter.* As soon as I—"

The crowd was booing. Down in the ring, the matador had made a poor *estocada.* The bull, now mortally wounded, the sword sticking out of its back, staggered drunkenly towards the side of the ring. It fell against the ***barrera,*** and slid to the ground. Even on the sand, it struggled to hold up its head, refusing to die. The matador had to kill it ignominiously with the dagger-like ***puntilla.*** The crowd booed even louder and began throwing programs and cushions into the ring.

Mason put his hand on Lisa's arm. "Look, Lisa, as soon as I woke up and knew where I was, the first thing I did was call the ***Schwartzer Bock.*** But you had checked out. So, I went to the ***Mutter Engel*** and—"

Lisa lifted her eyes and looked at him. "You went to the ***Mutter Engle?"***

"Yes. I talked to the maitre d' there. He told me about how you had waited and...and...Mason put his head in his hands. "Jesus, it was like someone had just punched me in the gut. The thought of you sitting there alone waiting for me, and then I don't show up." He put his hand on hers. "Lisa, I felt so awful. I never felt so awful in my life. It was—"

The crowd was cheering again. The second bull of the ***corrida*** had just chased another peone behind the **burladero.** This time it was the ***peone*** of the bullfighter everyone had come to see: the tiny matadora from Andalusia who was now standing in the shade behind the ***barrera*** waiting to step out onto the golden sand and make Spanish history in the ***Plaza de Toros.***

Out in the ring, the huge bull was snorting and pawing the ground. Ovilia Maria, the ***capea*** over her arm, slipped out from the ***barrera.*** Before she had taken a dozen steps, the bull charged. Ovilia Maria was ready. In one smooth, unhurried motion, she swept the lunging animal past her with a swirl of her ***capea.*** Shouts of ***Ole!*** rippled through the stands. The bull charged again. Again Ovilia Maria was ready and drew the massive head past her into the folds of the ***capea.*** For several minutes, the tiny matadora dazzled the crowd with one exciting cape pass after another, each time bringing the deadly horns closer and closer to her small, vulnerable body. Everyone in the stands was shouting ***Ole!*** She made another graceful pass, a beautifully slow ***veronica,*** then let the ***capea*** fall loosely at her side. She walked up to the bull, and for a moment, stood facing him only a few feet from his horns. Then she turned her back and walked contemptuously away. As the crowd rose to its feet, cheering, she returned to the ***barrera,*** handed the ***capea*** to her ***peone,*** and took the ***niutela*** and sword. She stepped back from the ***barrera,*** saluted the *Presidente,* and dedicated the bull to the cheering crowd. Then, throwing her *montera* on the sand, she strode out into the center of the ring, ready to begin the final act of the contest: the *faena de muleta.*

Lisa was looking at Mason. "Oh, Steve, I feel like such a fool. All the time I thought that...that...it was just that I was looking forward so much to having dinner with you, and...I had never asked a man to have dinner with me before…ever…and…and when you did not come, I just…" She began to cry.

Mason put his arms around her. "Come on, don't cry. I can't stand to see you cry." He took his handkerchief and wiped away her tears. "Come on, Lisa, please." He squeezed her shoulder and smiled at her. "Come on, you won't be able to see Ovilia Maria perform if you're crying."

Below in the ring, it was the moment of truth. The crowd was hushed. The bull, blood streaming from the wounds made by the *picador's* pike, pawed the ground, his whole massive body throbbing with pain and anger. Only a few feet away, Ovilia Maria stood poised, the *muleta* in one hand, the thin matador's sword in the other. Her colorful suit of lights was smeared with blood. The bull was now more dangerous than ever. He knew his enemy was not the *capea.*

He lowered his horns and charged. The tiny matadora stood like a statue until the huge snorting head was within inches of her chest. Then, as the crowd gasped, she snapped the *muleta* in his face and lunged forward with the sword, her slender body spinning up and over the deadly horns. The bull tried to turn and hook her from the side, but she was not there. His front legs buckled and he fell to his knees. Ovilia Maria danced away, holding only the *muleta.* The sword was planted squarely beween the bull's shoulders. She had performed the difficult *estocada a recibir,* making the bull charge onto the sword himself. The huge animal tried to stand up, stumbled and fell, collapsing in a cloud of dust in the sand. He rolled over on his side, gave a final shudder, then lay still. Ovilia Maria threw her arms in the air and strutted around the ring. The crowd went crazy.

Mason kissed Lisa on the forehead. "How about asking me to have dinner with you tonight?" He smiled at her. "I promise you I'll be there." He took her hand in his. "Because this time, I'm not going to let you out of my sight for one minute."

The trumpet sounded.

The ***Presidente*** rose in his box. He paused for a moment, then gave a signal with his hand. The whole arena erupted in cheers. He had awarded Ovilia Maria both of the bull's ears.

* * *

Mason smiled at Lisa across the candle-lit table. "Okay, what am I going to have for dessert?

Lisa was studying the menu. "Do you feel like having something sweet or—" She caught herself and laughed. "I know, I know; you are going to have whatever I have." She looked at him. "But all I am going to have is some fruit and cheese. You may want—"

"That sounds great to me," He signaled the waiter. "But let's have some more wine."

Lisa put her menu down and then reached across the table to put her hand on his. "Thanks for coming to Madrid."

He took her hand in his. "I'm glad I found you; I—" He lifted her hand and kissed it. For several moments, they sat looking into each other's eyes, not saying anything

Their table was tucked away in a small alcove under the winding stone steps that led down to the quaint wine cellar atmosphere of the old restaurant. The only other table in the alcove was empty. Mason looked around, then turned to Lisa. "This place, Botin, isn't it supposed to be famous for some reason?"

She nodded. "It was a favorite of Hemingway's. He came here after the bullfights with beautiful Spanish women."

Mason looked at her. "Well, he never came here with anyone as beautiful as you, I know that." Lisa's eyes smiled. The waiter brought the fruit and cheese and two glasses of wine. Lisa cut a slice from one of the pears and handed it to Mason. She started to cut another slice, then paused. He could see she was troubled about something. "What's the matter?"

"It's just that I'm worried, Steve."

"About what?"

"About that man who is following you. Do you have any idea why he is doing that?"

"No." Mason laughed. "That's what I was trying to find out when I got zonked."

"Could it have something to do with the case you are working on? I mean could he be working for the other chemical company, what's its name?"

"You mean Chimique?" He shook his head. "No, I don't think so. Parties in lawsuits don't usually hire people to follow the lawyers around."

Lisa took a sip of her wine. "Maybe—" She hesitated. "Maybe it has something to do with me."

Mason gave her a surprised look. "With you? Why would it have anything to do with you?"

She lowered her voice to a whisper. "For almost a year now, someone has been following me. It has not always been the same person. It has been different men at different times. But I am sure they were following me."

"How are you sure?"

"Oh, I am sure all right. The first time was about a year ago, in Paris, while I was shopping. I noticed this man, a short man with a beard, following me everywhere I went. I thought at first it was simply a coincidence that he just happened to be in the same stores. But then, when I was going home, there he was in the same Metro car with me."

"What did you do?"

"I deliberately got off the train at the wrong stop. I started walking toward the escalator up to the street. Then, just as the doors to the train were closing, I turned, ran back, and got on the Metro again."

"What did he do?

"He had also gotten off and headed toward the escalator. When he saw what I did, he tried to rush back and get on the train again too. But the doors had already closed and he was left at the station."

Mason nodded. "He was following you all right."

"Then, another time, when I was in London, someone went through my room at the hotel. They made an effort to put everything back, but I could tell someone had been there. Nothing was taken, and I had some jewelry in the room that would have been taken if it were a burglary." She paused. "No, whoever it was, they were looking for something else I am sure."

"Do you have any idea why someone would want to follow you, or go through your stuff?"

She took another sip of her wine. "I think I do." Mason did not say anything She looked at him. "I think it has to do with my father."

Mason again gave her a surprised look. "Your father?"

"Yes. He was in the ***Wehrmacht*** during the war. As I told you, Steve, he is not my real father but has been like a father to me and—" She looked around to make sure no one could overhear her. "He was born in Alsace but his parents were from Germany and he always thought of himself as Gelman. In the thirties, before the war, he went back to Germany and joined the army. He believed that Germany had been unfairly treated after the first World War, and he wanted to be part of making her strong again. He told me many times how much he loved Germany." She paused. "But he said he would never have gone back if he had known what Hitler was really like. He was very much against Hitler. He was one of those who joined the plot to kill him in 1944. When the plot failed, my father had to run away from the anny and hide from the Gestapo who were rounding up anyone even suspected of being implicated. It was when he was hiding from the Gestapo that he found me in a little village the Allies had bombed."

The waiter returned to ask if they wanted anything else. They each ordered a brandy. Then Lisa continued her story. "I know it seems that everyone now says they were against Hitler. But my father really was, Steve, he really was. After the war, his case was reviewed at the Nuremburg Trials and he was completely exonerated. Once, he showed me a document he received from the court at Nuremburg stating that he had not participated in any war crimes or anything like that. He was a soldier and he fought for Germany, that is true. But he hated the Nazis. He would never have been part of the awful things they did, I just know that." She paused. "You have to believe that, Steve."

"So, who do you think is following you?"

She frowned. "I am not sure. I know there are secret organizations made up of ex-Nazis and Nazi sympathizers who still believe all that stuff Hitler was preaching, and it may be them that—"

"What about the Israelis, you know, one of those groups that are always hunting down ex-Nazis, and—" He caught himself. "I don't mean your father was a Nazi. I believe you when you say he wasn't. I just mean—"

She shook her head. "No. The Israelis always make sure they have evidence the person they are after did something wrong." She paused. "When I first knew I was being followed and suspected it had something to do with my father, I thought it might be the Israelis too.

I wrote to Israel, to Golda Meir, and sent her a copy of the document my father had been given at Nuremburg."

"Did you get a reply?"

"Yes. Golda Meir herself wrote to me. She denied, of course, that she had any communication with any of the organizations I had referred to, but I'm sure she did. Anyway, she assured me I was not being followed by any Israeli organization. She said 'it was her understanding' the proceedings at Nuremburg were closely examined by such organizations and none of them would be interested in someone like my father who had been exonerated."

Mason sipped his brandy. "Is your father safe now where heis?"

"Yes, quite safe. He is in an old soldiers home in Metz. No one would think of looking for him there; it is a home for French soldiers."

"French soldiers?"

She smiled. "Yes. Remember, my father grew up in Alsace and has many family ties and friends there. He is using the name Marcel, Henri Marcel. His real name is Hans Molte."

Mason drank the rest of his brandy all in one swallow. "How come your name is Helms?"

"That is my real name My father learned it form the people in the village where he found me. He told me it was my real name and said I should keep it. I don't know if that was his real reason or—" She stopped because the maitre d' was seating someone at the other table in the alcove.

The two people being seated, a man and his wife, were obviously tourists. She was carrying a plastic shoulder bag stuffed with travel folders and guide books. He was loaded down with cameras, bandoleers of lenses, and other photographic paraphernalia.

Lisa turned to Mason. "You have not told me very much about yourself, Steve. I know you are a lawyer and that you are with a big law firm in Boston, Massachusetts, but—"

Mason laughed. "There really isn't that much to tell. I was born in France but my father was killed in the war, and my mother brought me to the United States when I was still just a baby. She died before I was two years old, and the foster family I was sent to live with adopted me, and they raised me after that. I grew up in a small town outside Boston and went to school there. Then I went away to college, spent four years there, and—" He made a face. "Sounds kind of dull, huh?"

She shook her head. "No, I am very interested; keep going."

"Well, after college, I got married, went in the service for a few years, came back, got divorced, kicked around for a while doing different things, then decided to go to law school. After law school, I went to work for old Whitaker, Brown, Thorndike and Templeton, where I've been since." He smiled. "And that's about it."

"What was her name?"

"Who?"

"Your wife."

"Marilyn."

"Were you very much in love with her?"

Mason shrugged. "Oh, I suppose I was at the time, yes." He paused. "I think we were both just too young, though. Anyway, that was a long time ago."

"Is there anyone—"

"Anyone now?"

"Yes."

He looked at her over the top of his empty brandy glass but did not say anything

She frowned. "There is someone, isn't there?

"Do you want an honest answer to that?"

She looked at him and nodded.

"The answer is yes."

She turned away and started to look out across the room.

He reached over, took her hand in his, and made her look at him. "It's someone I met just a few months ago." He let go of her hand and leaned back. "You won't believe this but we just bumped into each other one night we were both having dinner at the Pied de Cochon in Paris."

A flashbulb popped!

At the next table, the man was standing up waiting for his Polaroid picture to develop. He showed it to the woman with him and they both laughed. Then she stood up and took his picture; and they both laughed again. The man turned to Mason. "Par don nay seen yor."

Mason smiled. "Sony, I'm not Spanish; I'm an American."

The man's face broke into a broad grin. "Well, I'll be damned! Fellow Arnericanos, huh? And I took you for just a couple of Spaniards." He looked at Lisa. "Oh, pardon me, miss, I mean if you're Spanish and...Oh hell, if you're Spanish, why am I talking to you in English; I—"

Lisa interrupted him. "It's all right; I understand English."

The man beamed. "Well, what do you know, a couple of fellow Americans!" He turned to Mason. "Say, where are you all from in the good old U S of A, anyway?"

Mason smiled. "Boston."

"From Boston, huh? That's way up there in that little state of Massachusetts, isn't it?" He threw his shoulders back and stuck out his hand. "I'm from...I mean the little lady and me—this is my wife, Helen; we're from Dallas, down in the great state of Texas. And are we having a ball! Is this your first trip to Spain?"

Mason let the man shake his hand. "Yes."

"Well, it's ours too. And like I said, we're having a real ball. Take this place, for example; do you know who used to come here all the time? Ernest Hemingway, you know, the writer. I'll bet he sat at one of these tables right here."

Mason smiled politely. "We're just leaving. But it's been nice meeting you Mr.—"

"Hollister, George Hollister, that's my name. And this is my wife, Helen." He continued to pump Mason's hand. "We're staying at the—"

Mason cut him off. "Well, as I said, we're just leaving. I hope you enjoy your meal and the rest of your stay here." He turned to Lisa. "Are we all set?"

Lisa was already looking for the waiter to call for the check. She nodded to Mason and they both started to get up from the table.

Hollister put his hand on Mason's shoulder. "Aw, you don't really have to leave, do you?"

Mason stood up. "I'm afraid we do."

Hollister fumbled with his camera. "Look, before you go, will you—" He took the camera from around his neck . "Will you take a picture of me and Helen, you know, sitting here at the table together?" He handed Mason the camera. "It's all set; all you have to do is press that little button there." He started to sit down beside his wife, then stopped and put up his hand. "Wait a minute!" He took off his jacket and draped it over his shoulders, then sat down. "Okay, fire away!"

Mason took their picture. He waited for the film to slide out of the camera, then handed it back to Hollister.

Hollister watched the picture develop. "Hey, this is coming out great! I look just like Hemingway." He stood up. "Now, I'll take your picture, the two of you together."

Mason was about to shake his head, then changed his mind and smiled. "Okay, why not?" He sat down beside Lisa and whispered to her. "Let him take our picture and then let's get out of here."

She whispered back. "Yes."

Mason held up his hand "Wait a minute!" He jumped up, took off his jacket, and slipped it over his shoulders. Then he sat down again He put his arm around Lisa and smiled at her. "Okay, kid, get ready to have your picture taken with Ernest Hemingway."

Lisa leaned over and kissed him.

Hollister snapped the picture.

* * *

It was warm in the room. They had kicked off the covers and were lying together naked, their bodies glistening with perspiration but now relaxed. Mason was on his side, his arm cradling Lisa's head on the soft pillow. She was snuggled up close to him, her small but well developed breasts pressing against his chest, her long legs wrapped around his muscular thighs Mason, no longer hard, was still inside her and they were both still breathing heavily. He lifted his head and saw she was smiling. "What are you smiling at?"

She continued making lazy circles with her forger in the hair on his chest. "Was I smiling?"

"Yes. Tell me why?"

"Do I have to have a reason?"

He kissed her on the breast. "Sure, you've got to have a reason."

She pursed her lips and pretended to think about it. "I guess it's because I am so happy."

He ran his finger slowly around the nipple of her breast. "Do you know what?"

"What?"

He ran his finger up and over her chin and placed the tip of it on her nose. "You are the most beautiful person in the world."

Her eyes smiled. She pulled him down to her and kissed him. "I love you, Steve."

"I love you too." He kissed her, then whispered in her ear. "When I lost you in Wiesbaden, I thought I would die. It was as if someone had cut a piece out of me somewhere and—"

She smiled. "I felt the same way when you did not come to the restaurant."

They snuggled together and for several minutes lay there holding each other tightly. Then she looked up at him again. "Steve?"

"What?"

"I want to..." She paused. "I want to take you to see my father; I want him to meet you."

Mason looked down at her. He smiled, then kissed her again.

* * *

Mason tore the last day of May off his desk calendar. He crumpled it into a ball and tossed it over his shoulder at the waste basket in the corner. It missed completely. He shook his head and smiled, then turned his attention to the file Dietz had given him listing the sales managers still to be interviewed. Each one was marked with an M or a D. The important ones had all been done now, and he and Dietz had decided to handle the rest separately. The Hoch engineer was away this week interviewing the ones in Hamburg and Wilhelmshaven. Mason picked up the telephone and dialed Lisa's apartment. After two rings, she answered. "Hello?"

"Hi. I hope I'm not disturbing the muse."

She laughed. "No. As a matter of fact, I was just taking a break and making myself some coffee." She paused. "There is enough for two if you want to jump in a taxi and come over."

Mason groaned. "You temptress! You know there's nothing I'd rather do. But I can't. Dietz left a ton of stuff I've got to review before he gets back, and I have to get ready for a conference tomorrow with some French lawyers who are coming to see me.

That's why I thought I'd better call you today, to make sure we're all set for Saturday."

"Are we still meeting as planned?"

"Yes, I'll be waiting for you outside the *Chateau de*

Vincennes Metro stop at ten o'clock. As an extra precaution against being followed, I've rented a car. Everyone here thinks I'm taking my Porsche and driving alone out to see Mont St. Michel."

"What kind of car did you get, Steve?"

"A Citroen. They told me it would be a blue one."

"Okay, I'll look for you in a blue Citroen."

"See you then, kid."

"Good-bye, Steve. *Je t'aime.*" She hung up.

Mason sat for moment thinking. Then he looked again at the sales managers file to see which one to interview next.

* * *

It was Sunday and the historic old town of Verdun was just waking up. The church bells were welcoming the early risers to Mass. Through the open doors of the church, Mason and Lisa could hear organ music floating across the street to where they were sitting enjoying their croissants and coffee. It was a pleasant June day and the maitre d' had seated them at one of the outdoor tables in front of the hotel where they were staying.

Mason poured Lisa more coffee. "What time does your father expect us?"

"I usually try to get there around ten."

Mason looked up at the cloudless blue sky. "Well, it's certainly a perfect day for a picnic. Where are we going?"

"There is a park about a half hour's ride from Metz where my father likes to go if the weather is nice. It has a little pond and lots of flowers. My father loves flowers. He has,a small garden at the soldiers' home that he will want to show you, and you should make a fuss over it. He is very proud of it."

"I think the most beautiful flowers I've ever seen were at the *Keukenhof* in Holland. Have you ever been there?"

"Yes, it is one of my favorite places."

"What's your favorite place of all"

"You mean anywhere?"

"Yes. I mean, where would you go if you could just go anywhere you wanted?"

"She thought for a moment. "The Isle of Capri."

"What's that like?"

She smiled. "I have never been there."

"Oh?"

"I have always wanted to go there, but—"

"But what?"

"But...well...it is not a place I want to go...I mean go with just anyone." She blushed slightly. It's a place I'm saving until..." She looked at him. "...until the right person has come along to go there with me."

It was Mason's turn to blush. For several moments he did not say anything He looked at her and saw her smiling, almost laughing "What's funny?"

"What you just did, Steve."

"What did I just do?"

"You ran your finger around the top of your ear while you were thinking. My father does the same thing when he is thinking about something I remember once, when I was a little girl, I asked him why he did it. He joked with me and said it was to slow down his mind so he would not say the wrong thing "

Mason laughed. "Well, your father was right. That's why I was doing it, so I wouldn't say the wrong thing "

Lisa smiled. "What were you going to say?"

Mason put his finger to his ear again and ran it back and forth, pretending to be thinking hard about what he was going to say. "I was going to say…I mean I was just thinking that sometime you and I—" He stopped. Lisa was mimicking him. She had put her finger on her ear and was rubbing it back and forth slowly, pensively. "I know now, Steve, that all my life I've been waiting…" Her eyes found his. "…to go to the Isle of Capri with you."

* * *

Mason walked up the knoll until he could see the little pond on the other side. He picked a shady spot under an old gnarled tree and spread the blanket down on the cool grass. For a minute he stood watching two small boys sailing a toy boat on the edge of the pond through a group of habitant ducks. Then he started back down to the Citroen to help Lisa and Molte with the food. As he walked toward them, he thought about the strange feeling he had when he first met Molte at the soldiers' home, a feeling he had never experienced before. It was almost as if he already knew Molte, and had met him before somewhere. He decided it was just that the old man was exactly as he had pictured: his face lined with age but still strong and handsome, blue eyes touched with sadness but clear and alert; all the classic Teutonic features Mason had expected.

Lisa was closing the trunk of the car. "Okay, I have everything." She turned to Molte. "Papa, let Steve take the picnic basket; it is too heavy for you. You take the wine."

Molte put down the basket and picked up the wine. He shook his head, smiling. "I do not know what to say, Stephen. When she was a little girl, all she ever talked about was independence. She did not think people should take orders from anyone." He laughed. "Now she is grown up and gives me orders all the time." He continued to shake his head as they walked up to the top of the knoll.

They all sat down on the blanket, the two men waiting like schoolboys for Lisa to pass them their lunch from the basket. Molte twisted a cockscrew into one of the wine bottles. "Since I have been assigned the role of *sommelier*… "He popped the cork out of the bottle. "Here, *Fraulein* Helms, I give you the honor of deciding whether the vintage is suitable for your guests, *Herr* Mason and me." He winked at Mason.

Lisa ignored him. "Papa, I told Steve about the men who have been following me. Now someone is following him as well."

A troubled expression came over Molte's face. "Someone has been following you, Stephen?"

"Yes. I don't know who he is. He's a big guy, always wears a gray vest. I can't figure out why the hell he's following me."

Lisa turned to Molte. "I think it has to do with us, Papa; I think he is another of those who are trying to find you."

Molte nodded. "Yes, that could be." He looked at Mason. "As Lisa may have told you, I was involved with the Stauffenberg group that tried to rid Germany of Hitler in 1944. All of that of course came out at Nuremburg, and as a result I became one of those marked for death by the Odessa

"The Odessa, isn't that a secret organization of fowler members of the SS and the Gestapo?"

"Yes. To hide from them, I changed my name to Marcel and bought a small farm out here in Alsace where I hoped to be able to live out the rest of my life in peace." He shook his head sadly. "I had all but forgotten being hunted by anyone. Then, about a year ago, Lisa came to me and said she was being followed."

"By the Odessa?"

"I am not sure. I find it hard to believe they are still after me. Look at me; I am almost eighty years old. Most of them, if they are still alive, are now old men too. And all of that was so long ago."

Lisa handed them both some bread and ham. "I told Steve we were certain it was not the Israelis, Papa. I explained to him about the document you were given at Nuremburg, and about the letter I received from Golda Meir."

Mason held out his glass so Molte could pour him some more wine. "Do you think it could be some Israeli fringe group that thinks you shouldn't have been exonerated at Nuremburg?"

Molte nodded. "I suppose that is a possibility, yes." He looked at Mason. "But I tell you this, Stephen; the Jews have no quarrel with me. I was no Nazi. I hated the Nazis. They were nothing but hoodlums, street hoodlums who seized on Germanys' misfortune after the First World War and dragged her down even deeper into disaster. No, Stephen, if it is Jews who are after me, they are misguided."

They fmished their lunch, and Lisa suggested to her father that they take a walk around the pond. She turned to Mason. "Are you coming, Steve?"

"No, thanks. You two go; you should have some time together alone. I'll just lie here and contemplate the sky for a while."

Lisa slipped her arm inside Molte's and they left.

Mason stretched out on the blanket and put his hands behind his head. He closed his eyes. Maybe what I should do is just come right out and ask Molte if he's ever heard of Kopt. He shook his head. No, I can't do that. He frowned. One thing is clear, though; there's something fishy about Kopt. But what the hell is he up to? Mason opened his eyes. The sky was a brilliant blue, not a cloud anywhere. He closed his eyes again. Come on, Mason, you're a lawyer; analyze the situation; break it down the way you'd break down a case you were preparing for trial. Okay, let's start with Kopt. There's something phony about his story; it just doesn't hang together. So, lets take it step by step. Suppose he's not an Israeli at all, that he's really a Nazi or Nazi sympathizer and just pretending to be an Israeli. If that's so, everything he told me about the concentration camp and about working for Israel, was all a lie. Mason shook his head. No, I'm sure he was telling the truth about that. Besides, Templeton checked it out that Kopt had all sorts of connections in Israel. No, Kopt's an Israeli all right. That's fact one. So why is he giving me all this business about the Israeli's wanting to find Molte? If Molte was exonerated at Nuremburg, why would the Israelis—" He caught himself Wait a minute, Mason; how do you know that Molte really was exonerated? What if it's Lisa and Molte who aren't telling the truth? Okay, so you can't believe that Lisa would lie to you. But what if she thought she was protecting her father; then she would, wouldn't she? Come on, Mason, think like a lawyer. Okay, so maybe she'd lie to protect him; no one could blame her for that. But why lie to me? How could lying to me protect him. She doesn't know why I'm over here. He shook his head. No, the key to this whole thing is Kopt; it's got to be. So, where are we? First, Kopt's an Israeli, that's fact one. But he's not trying to find Molte for Israel; that's fact two. So, either he's tied in with some fringe group or he's

"Steve? Are you sleeping, Steve?"

Mason opened his eyes, and saw that Lisa and Molte had returned. He looked up at them and smiled. "No, I was just daydreaming a little." He sat up. "How was your walk?

"It was nice. Papa was just saying what a perfect day it is."

Molte looked at Mason. "Stephen, there is something I want to say to you, now, so Lisa too can hear." He sat down on the blanket. "Lisa has known other men, of course. She was even married for a brief time." He looked at her, then continued. "We have always been close, Lisa and I. Ever since that day when I found her, a little girl crying in a pile of rubble, and picked her up in my arms." He reached over and took Lisa's hand in his. "Now I am almost eighty years old and—"

"Papa! Stop talking about how old you are. You will probably live to be—"

He cut her off "No, it is important Stephen hear what I have to say." He turned to Mason again. "If you only knew how much I have hoped and prayed that someday, before I died, Lisa would find someone, someone she truly loved, and who truly loved her."

Lisa reached over and took Molte's hand in both of hers. "I have found him, Papa; all you have hoped and prayed for has come true. I love Steve, and he loves me. I have never been so happy."

For several minutes none of them said anything. Then Mason turned and looked out over the pond. Behind him, he could hear the old man weeping.

* * *

Monday morning, on his way to the office, Mason stopped at the bank and drew another twenty thousand francs on his letter of credit. Then he went to see the firm's travel agent on the *Champs Elysees.* By the time he reached the office, it was almost eleven o'clock.

"Good morning, *monsieur.*"

"Good morning, Nadine."

The little secretary smiled. "How did you like *Mont St. Michel?* Did you have an omelet while you were there?"

Mason shook his head. "I'm afraid I passed up the omelet. Has Mr. Dietz been looking for me?

"Yes, he is quite anxious to see you."

"Tell him I'm ready to meet with him whenever he wants." He paused. "And, oh yes, another thing—"

"Yes, *monsieur?*"

"I want to talk to Mr. Templeton in Boston as soon as I can." Mason looked at his watch. "It's still too early over there now. The office opens at eight-thirty, their time. Put the call in as soon as you can after that. If Mr. Templeton's not there, leave word at the switchboard that I called and want to speak with him as soon as he comes in."

Nadine nodded. "I understand, ***monsieur.***"

Mason walked down to his office, and sat down at his desk. A moment later, Dietz poked his head in the door. "Hi, Steve, what's new?"

"Come in, Carl. How was your week in Germany?

Dietz pulled a chair up close to Mason's desk. "Which part, the business or the pleasure?"

"Give me the business first."

"I'm afraid I didn't get very much, I—" Dietz smiled. "You understand I'm talking about the business part now."

Mason laughed. "Yeah, I understand.".

The Hoch engineer became serious. "It wasn't a total waste of time I got the names of a few former Hoch salesmen who should be able to give us some information on Chimique's activities in Germany But the two guys I interviewed couldn't give me anything first hand. They're both new sales managers and everything we want to know happened before they came with the company." He paused. "How about your week? Did you learn anything helpful?"

Mason shook his head. "Not really. I met with the French lawyers about getting some help from the courts here if we want to take depositions of those guys in our Glasgow Office."

"What did the French lawyers say?"

Mason smiled. "Just what American lawyers would say, that they need to research the matter before they can give any opinion. But it sounds like it's going to turn out the way I thought. Until we start an actual lawsuit, we're pretty much out of luck."

"After we start the lawsuit, though, then we can do it?"

"Not necessarily. We still have to go before the French court and ask for Letters Rogatory."

"What the hell are they?"

"They're a formal request by the French court asking the British court to compel the guys in Glasgow to submit to our depositions." "If the French court gives us the Letters...whatever they are, then what happens?"

"Then we take them over and try to persuade the British court to honor them."

Dietz frowned. "You mean we have to persuade two different courts, first the one here in France, then the one in England?"

"That's right."

"And we can't even start until we've got a lawsuit going?"

Mason shrugged. "I'm not sure about that. That's what I was talking to the French lawyers about. They say there may be a procedure we can use to get the depositions ahead of time, on the grounds we'll lose our chance if we don't do it now. That's the question they're researching. They promised to get back to me next week." He buzzed for Nadine and asked her to bring some coffee. Then he looked at Dietz and smiled. "Okay, now tell me about the other part of your trip. I know you're dying to tell me."

Dietz laughed. "That's a different story; that was a real success. Wilhelmshaven wasn't much, but that Hamburg was something else. Remember the section we went to in Amsterdam? Well, in Hamburg, they've got—"

Nadine interrupted him with the coffee. She put it on Mason's desk. "I spoke to our switchboard, ***monsieur,*** and told them to call the Boston Office at one-thirty. I told them you wanted to talk to Mr. Templeton as soon as possible, that it is very important."

Dietz's eyes followed her as she left. He turned to Mason. "That's a cute little ass on that Nadine. I love the way she wiggles it when she walks." He sat back in his chair, balancing his coffee cup on his cast. "By the way, how are things going with that girl you mentioned, you know, the one that writes articles or something?"

"Fine. As a matter of fact, we're going to Italy together next week-end. She's always wanted to go to the Isle of Capri, and—"

"The Isle of Capri!" Dietz laughed. "Sounds pretty serious to me. Don't tell me old Steve has fallen in love?"

Mason smiled. "Well, things like that happen, you know." He opened the file on his desk. "I've checked the list of sales managers still to be interviewed, and there's one in Salerno. I thought I'd go and interview him first and then drive on to Naples."

Dietz jokingly pointed at the file. "The guy in. Salerno, thought his name had a D beside it?"

Mason looked at him. "It's got an M now." They both laughed. "But don't feel too bad, I gave you the one in Nice instead." "Nice for Salerno; I can't complain about that! Are you going to take the girl to Salerno with you?"

Mason shook his head. "No, she's coming from—" He caught himself. "No, she's flying down and meeting me in Naples."

Dietz laughed. "I've been to Naples, Steve. Be careful there, or they'll steal the shirt right off your back. What hotel are you staying at in Salerno, anyway?"

"I don't know yet. I'll leave the name with Nadine I'll also leave the names of the hotels in Naples and Capri, so you can reach me if you need to."

Dietz finished his coffee, and put his empty cup on the desk. He stood up. "Okay, but it'll have to be something pretty important before I'll interrupt romance on the Isle of Capri."

Mason laughed. "How about lunch today?"

Dietz shook his head. "I can't, Steve. I'd like to but I've got an appointment with the doctor to see how this arm is coming along. What about tomorrow?"

"Sure." Mason pointed to Dietz's cast. "You must be getting sick of that thing by now. When is it supposed to come off, anyway?" Dietz shrugged. "I don't know. Soon, I hope."

* * *

It was just a few minutes after one-thirty. Mason got up from his desk and walked out to see how Nadine was doing with the call to Boston. The little secretary had the telephone crooked in her shoulder, listening "The operator is talking to Boston now, ***monsieur.*** They are getting Mr. Templeton for you." She listened some more, then looked up at Mason. "They have him now, ***monsieur;*** he is on the line."

"Okay, Nadine, hang up. I'll take it in my office." He hurried back into his office, closed the door, and picked up the phone of his desk. "Hello, Mr. Templeton?"

"Yes, hello, Steve."

"Can you hear me all right?"

"Yes, go ahead."

"I hope I haven't picked a bad time to ask you to call. There's something I need to talk to you about, and it's going to take a while to explain."

"No, this is a good time, Steve. Is there some problem?" Mason sat down at his desk. "I'm afraid there is. I've been struggling to solve it myself, but I need your advice."

All right, Steve." Templeton's voice was calm. "Take your time. Tell me what the problem is."

Mason paused for a moment. "Well, to start with, I'm convinced Kopt has lied to me. I don't mean just about something minor; I mean about this whole assignment I'm supposed to have over here."

"Are you sure?"

"No. I mean that's part of the problem."

"Go on, Steve."

"It's more than just that I don't think I'm here for the purpose he told me. I think his real purpose is a sinister one."

"What do you mean by 'sinister?'"

"I mean I think he's using me to fmd someone and that—" He lowered his voice. "That when I fmd him, Kopt is going to have him killed." Mason could hear Templeton take a deep breath.

"Steve?"

"Yes?"

"I think you'd better tell me what your assignment is over there."

"But—"

"I know. I know what our agreement is with Kopt. But if he's lied to you, and if someone's life may be involved, I think we've got to bend that agreement a little and—"

Mason interrupted him. "But I'm not really sure he is lying. And if he isn't, we haven't got any reason to break our agreement." He paused. "What I'd like to do is start telling you the whole story, and have you stop me if you think that—"

"Go ahead."

"Well, first, you know that all this Hoch versus Chimique business is just a cover story."

"I guessed as much."

"My real assignment over here is to help find a foimer Gelman army officer that Israel has been looking for since World War II. His name is Molte and he's supposed to be some sort of war criminal that's hiding here in France."

"Hinmm. Strikes me as rather an unusual assignment for a trial lawyer, Steve."

"That's what my reaction was when Kopt first told me about it at the Ritz. He said he picked me because Lisa—I mean Molte's daughter—wait a minute, I'm getting ahead of myself; let me back up." He paused. "Molte has a daughter, Lisa, living here in Paris. She knows where he is. According to Kopt, the Israelis have made several attempts to get her to lead them to her father, but they have all failed because she knows they're after him, and is on her guard. My assignment is to get to know her, make friends with her, and find out where her father is. The information will then be turned over to the Israelis. Kopt assured me the only reason they want to fmd Molte is to expose him. He said I was picked for the job because the last person in the world Lisa would suspect is a Boston trial lawyer."

"Hmmm. I have to admit that last part makes a certain amount of sense."

"That's what I thought, too. And it's worked out just that way. I'm sure Lisa has no idea I'm over here to fmd out where her father is."

Templeton cleared his throat. "I gather from what you say, Steve, that you've already been successful in making friends with this Lisa and—"

"I'm afraid I've done more than that."

There was silence on the other end of the line. Templeton cleared his throat again. "You mean the relationship has become more than platonic."

"Yes. And I'm concerned that it may be clouding my judgment in the matter."

"Hmmm. It could be, of course. On the other hand, if you're right about Kopt's real purpose, then we have a situation where a man's life is at stake."

"That's why I thought I'd better talk to you, and get your advice."

"I'm glad you did." There was a pause. "Tell me, Steve, what is it this Molte is supposed to have done that Israel is so interested in finding him?"

"That's it. I don't think Israel's interested in him at all. For one thing, he wasn't a Nazi; he was just an ordinary soldier that—" Mason interrupted himself know, they all say they weren't Nazis. But I've seen a document he was given at the Nuremburg trials exonerating him of any war crimes. I've also seen a letter from Golda Meir saying that Israel isn't interested in him. Both documents could be forgeries but I don't think so." He paused. "And another thing: some guy's been following me since I got over here. I don't know who the hell he is. At first, I thought he might be someone trying to protect Molte. But now, I'm convinced he's working for Kopt."

"Have you found out where this Molte is?"

"He's in a home for French soldiers in Metz, living under an assumed name."

"You know, Steve, I haven't liked this whole Kopt business from the beginning But I think we have to go slowly. I tell you what. For the time being, don't do anything. Take a few days off and go somewhere, away from Paris. In the meantime, I'll make a few inquiries here and see what I can fmd out."

"Okay. I was planning to take a little time off next week anyway. I'm going to Italy for a few days. I'll hold off making any report to Kopt until

I get back, and have a chance to talk to you again."

"When will you be back?"

"A week from today."

"Fine. I'll see what I can fmd out between now and then. When you get back, call me."

"I will. And thanks."

"I want you to be careful, Steve."

"I understand."

They both hung up.

Three buildings away, at 13 ***Avenue Anatole France,*** the two clicks could be heard distinctly in his earphones. As soon as he heard them, Sieg disconnected his tap.

* * *

Little is known about the Etruscans and Carthaginians who settled along the mountainous west coast of central Italy thirty centuries ago. And why they chose such inhospitable terrain remains a mystery to this day. Seafarers by nature, they became, of necessity, a race of cave dwellers, literally carving their homes into the sides of the formidable mountains that rise up sharply from the inland plains and then plunge precipitously in sheer vertical cliffs down to the Mediterranean below.

Almost all evidence of the ancient civilization has now disappeared, a few crumbled artifacts can still be seen on the spectacular Amalfi Drive that winds treacherously along a narrow ledge high up on the perpendicular wall of the rugged mountain between Salerno and Sorrento.

Mason could have driven inland and taken the flat, four-lane *autostrada* to Naples. It would have been quicker. But the view of the Mediterranean offered by the Amalfi Drive was said to be one of the most spectacular in all Europe. It would have been a shame to miss it, he had decided. He was still only a few kilometers north of Salerno and even now, as his little rented Fiat wound its way up the side of the mountain, the view was breathtaking. The sparkling blue Mediterranean below stretched off in the distance as far as the eye could see. The afternoon sun, making its long lazy descent to the horizon, was painting everything a warm amber.

The road, one hairpin turn after another, was barely wide enough for two cars and Mason kept the little Fiat as close as he could to the steep wall of rock on his right. Along the outside of the ledge, on his left, a low stone wall served as a perfunctory guard rail. He swung over next to it and looked down. It was a straight drop of more than a thousand feet to the water below. He swung back to the right side of the road again.

The interview in Salerno had gone well. A few months ago, Chimique had tried to hire away one of Hoch's people there. Mason smiled to himself. He could still hear the *mafioso* Sales Manager telling him how Chimique had made a big mistake trying to raid a sales office in southern Italy. Everyone in the office was related and Chimique had picked the Sales Manager's nephew to approach. The nephew pretended to be interested, listened to everything the Chimique guy had to say, then beat the shit out of him, and reported the whole thing to his uncle. Mason glanced at the attache case on the seat beside him. And now it was all in the nice little affidavit the nephew had given him.

Mason was now high up on the side of the mountain. The hairpin turns were getting even sharper. The road ahead curved around a deep crevasse, then back out to a treacherous outside ledge. As he reached the outside ledge, he honked his horn, downshifted and cut sharply around the blind turn, hugging the steep wall of rock on his right. A car coming the other way whizzed past, gave him a friendly toot, and then disappeared behind him.

He came around the next outside ledge and his eyes widened. Coming towards him from the opposite direction, lumbering its way around the crevasse, was a big green and white Italian tour bus. He downshifted quickly. Holy Jesus! That big mother will never make it past me! He pulled the little Fiat over to the right as far as he could. The tour bus thundered past, scraping its outside wheels against the stone guard rail. Mason watched in the rear view mirror as the bus maneuvered around the narrow ledge and disappeared. Then he saw something else in the mirror: another car, a small black Alfa Romeo, coming up fast behind him. He swung in and around the next crevasse and looked back. The Alfa was still the same distance behind him; it had not gained on him at all. That's funny, he thought, the way I'm driving that Alfa should be climbing all over my ass.

He looked in the mirror again The driver of the Alfa Romeo was hunched low behind the steering wheel and had his hat pulled down over his forehead. But there was enough of his face showing. Mason bit his lip. That son of a bitch! He's even following me here too. That does it! It's time for an accounting with the bastard. He started taking the turns faster, more recklessly, sizing up each outside ledge as he swung in and around the crevasse before it. He decided the next one would be the one. He tightened his grip on the steering wheel. Okay, fella, this is it! He pressed down on the accelerator. The Fiat lunged toward the outside ledge ahead. Mason honked his horn and cut into the turn without downshifting. The tires of the Fiat squealed in protest as the little car leaned hard to the outside, almost hitting the stone guard rail, then swung back to the inside, taking the sharpest part of the turn without losing speed. As soon as he was around the ledge, Mason drove the Fiat against the side of the mountain, scraping it along the wall of rock to slow it down. Then he slammed on the brakes and stopped in the middle of the road. He jumped out, ran behind the Fiat and waited. His forehead was covered with sweat. He wiped it off with the back of his hand as he listened for the sound of the Alfa Romeo. He heard a different sound, from the opposite direction. He turned and looked. Coming the other way, lumbering around the next crevasse, was another Italian tour bus. Mason turned back toward the ledge. He could hear the Alfa Romeo now. Then suddenly it appeared, coming fast around the ledge, Gray Vest's face wide with surprise at seeing the Fiat stopped in the middle of the road in front of him. He was going too fast to stop. He cut to the right, missing the Fiat by inches and careening against the side of the mountain. He swerved back into the middle of the road, still going too fast. And now, directly in front of him, hissing as the driver frantically pumped his air brakes, was the big Italian tour bus. Gray Vest had no choice; the bus was too close to the side of the mountain; he had to try to pass it on the outside. The Alfa's tires squealed as it skidding sideways across the narrow ledge. It slammed into the low guard rail and bounced up in the air. It crashed back down on top of the guard rail and teetered there, its rear end hanging out over the edge of the cliff. Through the windshield he saw Gray Vest's face, twisted in honor, turn white as the Alfa began to slip backwards. His hands clawed at the window as it slipped back further, then slid off the guard rail and over the edge of the cliff.

The driver of the tour bus ran up beside Mason. They both looked down. The Alfa Romeo had already fallen several hundred feet. Now only the size of a matchbox and still falling, it was twisting and turning in the air. Then it hit, and all around it the blue water exploded in a large white circle. Mason stepped back from the edge. "Jesus! What a way to go!"

The bus driver pointed down. "*Pazzo! Pazzo!* That man was crazy! He didn't have a chance of making it around me going that fast." He looked at Mason. "Who was he, do you know?"

Mason peered over the cliff. The white circle had disappeared; the water was blue and calm again. He shook his head. "No. Bit whoever the hell he was, he sure thought it was important that I didn't find out."

* * *

The Excelsior Hotel in Naples was experiencing another one-day strike by its employees. None of its bellmen, waiters, bartenders or other staff had reported for work. No demand had been made for higher wages or better working conditions, and the employees would all be back at their jobs tomorrow as a matter of course. But today, as an expression of independence, they were all standing across the street in mufti, staring sullenly at the front door of the hotel.

The concierge gave Mason is key. "I apologize, *signore,* but you will have to carry your luggage up to your room yourself." He paused. "And, oh yes, you received a telephone call from your office in Paris. They want you to call back right away." He handed Mason a slip of paper. Mason looked at it. The call was from Dietz.

"Where can I take the call?"

"I would suggest your room, *signore.* Our switchboard operator is not working today and I will have to put the call through for you. It will take a few minutes." He motioned Mason towards the elevator. "I will ring your room as soon as I have made the connection."

Mason had just taken off his jacket and thrown it on the bed when the telephone rang. It was the concierge. "I have your call to

Paris now, *signore.*"

Mason waited. Then he heard Dietz come on the line. "Steve?" "Hi, Carl. What's up?"

"Hi, Steve. Everything go okay in Salerno?"

"Fine. The hotel here said you wanted me to call you right away. Is there some problem?"

"Yeah, I think there is. I don't know what the hell it's all about, but it sounds like it might be serious. I thought you should know about it right away."

"Go ahead, Carl; I'm listening "

"You know that telephone call you made to Boston just before you left for Italy?"

"What about it?"

Mason heard Dietz take a breath. "It was tapped, Steve; someone was listening in on your conversation. I didn't know about it until Doucette came to see me. He found out about it and thought it had something to do with the case."

"Keep going."

"Doucette said he checked to find out where the tap was coming from and—"

"Did he find out?"

"The phone was listed to a *Monsieur* Mollet at a building down the street here."

"Who's he?"

"We figure it's just a phony name. Mollet's a common name here, you know, like Smith. The address is a shabby apartment building where people rent rooms by the week, or even by the day if they want."

"So we don't know who it was that—"

Dietz interrupted him. "Hang on, Steve, there's a lot more." "Okay, keep going."

Well, you know old Doucette. As soon as he found out where the tap was coming from, he had a tap put on that phone. He has a cousin or something in the telephone company and—"

"Then what?"

"After Doucette's tap was on, there was only one other call. It was to Tel Aviv."

"Tel Aviv!" Mason sat down on the bed.

"Yeah. Doucette had the conversation recorded and a transcript made. I have the transcript right in front of me. It wasn't a long conversation, and it doesn't make any sense to me."

"What was said?"

"Well, the first part was just the business with the over sea's operator. Then the person in Paris, this guy, Mollet, or whatever his name is, said—"

Mason interrupted him. "Do we know who he was talking to in Tel Aviv?"

"No. I've read the whole transcript carefully, Steve, and there's no mention of the guy's name anywhere."

"Okay. You were telling me what the guy in Paris said."

"Yeah. He said you had made a call to your Boston Office, and that you knew where someone named Molte was. That's M 0 L T E, Steve. The guy in Paris then said that this Molte was in a French soldiers' home in Metz, living under an assumed name. The guy in Tel Aviv asked what the assumed name was. The guy in Paris said he didn't know, that you hadn't mentioned it. The guy in Tel Aviv said it was not important, that the assumed name would not be a problem."

Dietz paused. "None of this makes any sense to me, Steve, who the hell is this guy, Molte anyway?"

"Keep going, Carl."

"Well, then the guy in Tel Aviv said—" Dietz stopped. "I'd better read this part to you. The guy in Tel Aviv said 'good work.' At last we finally have him."

Mason loosened his tie. "Did the guy in Tel Aviv say anything else after that?"

"Yeah. But I'll read it to you because it doesn't make any sense at all to me. He said 'Otto will leave for Metz right away; this is a job for—" Dietz paused. "Then there's a word I don't understand at all. I can't even pronounce it."

"Spell it."

"It's spelled S H C H E E T A. And that's it, Steve; after that they both hung up. What the hell is this all about, do you know? Steve? Are you still there?"

Mason was sweating; he could feel the wetness running down under his arms. "Yes, I'm still here."

"Who the hell is this guy, Molte, anyway?"

Mason hesitated, then made a decision. "He's Lisa's father."

"Lisa's father? I thought you told me her name was something else, I mean I didn't know that—"

Mason interrupted him. "I'll explain all that later. Right now, we've got to do something fast." He thought for a moment. "Carl?" "Yeah, Steve?"

"I need your help."

"Sure, anything What do you want me to do?"

"We've got to get Lisa's father out of that soldiers' home right away. They're going to kill him if we don't."

"Kill him! Who's going to kill him?"

"The guy in Tel Aviv. Don't ask me how I know; I just know. That guy, Otto he's sending to Metz is a trained killer. Let me think for a minute. It sounded like Otto was in Tel Aviv; but he could be anywhere. Christ! Let's hope he isn't as close to Metz as—" Mason paused. "How long will it take you to get to Metz if you leave right away?"

"I think I can make it in two hours, Steve, maybe less if the traffic is not too heavy."

Mason looked at his watch. "It's just two-thirty here; what is it there?"

"One-thirty. If I leave right away, I should be in Metz before four. Where do I go when I get to Metz?

"Go right through Metz. Follow the signs that say Thionville—that's T H I O N V I L L E. Gotit?"

"Yeah. Then what?"

"After you leave Metz, you'll go over a big bridge; you can't miss it. You'll then be on the road to Thionville. Keep watching on the right. About two kilometers after the bridge, you'll come down a steep hill and at the bottom there's a right turn you have to take. There's a sign there that says Marshall Foch Military something or other; you'll see it."

"What do I do when I get to the soldiers' home?"

Mason looked at his watch again. "Ask for Lisa, Lisa Helms. If she's not there, wait for her. She may be taking her father out for a drive. If she is, she'll be back sometime between four and five; she's planning to catch a six o'clock plane down here. As soon as you see her, get her and her father the hell out of there."

"What do I tell her?

"Tell her I sent you. She'll know who you are because I've told her all about the case we're working on. Tell her there's an Israeli agent on his way there to kill her father. Tell her anything you have to, but get them both the hell of there as fast as you can."

"Steve?"

'Yeah?"

"I just thought of something"

"What?"

"I think I know a place I can take them where they'll be safe." "Where?"

"I have an uncle who has a small farm about ninety kilometers from Metz. My aunt died a couple of years ago and he lives there alone now. His place is off in the woods, in the middle of nowhere. It's only a small place and they can't stay there forever; but it's someplace they can hide until they decided what to do next. And it's a place I can tell you how to get to, so you can meet us there." He paused. "Can you get a plane out of Naples this afternoon?"

"I don't know. As soon as we hang up, I'm going to call the airport. I'll have to fly to Strasbourg and drive from there; so it'll probably be several hours before I can get there. How do I get to your uncle's farm from Strasbourg?"

"When you get the car at the airport, ask them to give you directions to Bitche—B I T C H E. Bitche is about a hundred kilometers north of Strasbourg. It's only a small town but you'll see the signs for it."

"What do I do when I get to this Bitche?"

"My uncle's farm is just outside the town. It's on a long winding road that goes through the woods and leads down to an old Maginot Line fortress. When you get to Bitche, just ask someone how to get to. that."

"The old fortress, does it have a name?"

"Yeah," There was a pause. "It's called Simserhof."

* * *

The woman behind the Alitalia counter handed Mason his ticket. "Here you are, sir." She smiled. "Have a pleasant flight."

"Thanks." Mason saw that the flight was not scheduled to board for another half hour. He looked around for a telephone. He found one, took a slip of paper out of his pocket, spread it out on the narrow counter, and dialed.

A man's voice answered. "Allo?"

"Is this the *Marshal Foch Maison Militaire des Soldats?"* The voice switched to English. "Yes, what can I do for you?" "I'm calling about one of your residents, Henri Marcel; his daughter is a friend of mine. Is either of them there now?"

"No, *monsieur,* they both left about an hour ago." There was a pause. "Are you *Monsieur* Mason?"

"Yes, why?"

"There is a message here for you."

"What does it say?"

"It is a handwritten note. It says 'Carl is here, and has explained everything We are leaving with him now. Will meet you there. Please hurry. Love, Lisa.' Shall I read it again, *monsieur?"*

"No, I've got it. But there is something else."

"Yes, *monsieur?"*

Has anyone been there or called asking about Marcel?" You mean anyone else?"

"Yes"

"No, there has been no one."

Mason was relieved. He hung up the phone and looked at his watch. There was still twenty minutes before the plane boarded. He thought for a moment, then decided to call Doucette and fmd out if his tap had picked up any more calls. He dialed the Paris Office.

"*Bonjour.* Whitaker, Brown, Thomdike and Templeton."

"Hi. This is Mr. Mason. Is Mr. Doucette there?"

"Oh, hello, *Monsieur* Mason. Yes, I think he is still here. I'll ring his line for you."

Mason waited. Then he heard Doucette's voice. *"Alio?"* "Andre, its' Steve Mason."

"Monsieur Mason! How are you?"

"Fine, Andre, fine. I'm still at the airport in Naples. My plane's leaving in a few minutes. Dietz told me about the tap on the phone and—"

"—the tap, *monsieur?'*

"Yes, I'm calling to see whether you've picked up any more—" "But I—"

"You've still got the tap on, I hope."

"I do not understand, *monsieur."*

"The telephone tap, the one you put on the phone at the place down the street."

There was a pause.

"I'm sorry, *Monsieur* Mason, but I know nothing about any telephone tap."

Mason was aware of a strange feeling in his stomach. "Andre, listen to me."

"Yes, *monsieur?"*

"Last Friday, before I left for Italy, I made a call to Boston, to the Boston Office."

"Yes."

"Didn't you find out sometime afterwards that the call had been tapped, you know, that someone had listened in on—"

"I understand, *monsieur.* But no, I know nothing about any tap on your telephone."

Mason was puzzled. "Then why did you tell Dietz that—"

Doucette interrupted him. "I said nothing to *Monsieur* Dietz about any telephone tap. I have not even spoken to *Monsieur* Dietz since—oh, yes I did speak to him, his morning But he was in a hurry to leave and we spoke only briefly."

Mason could feel his whole body sweating now. "What did he say, anything?"

"He just said good-bye, that he would not be back for a few days. I a r.ri afraid, *monsieur,* that I did most of the talking. I saw that he fmally had his cast taken off. I had never seen him without it and—"

The sweat, now pouring down Mason's back turned ice cold. He knew what Doucette was going to say next."

CC—and *Monsieur* Mason, I had no idea his, hand was so badly injured. The middle fingers are all missing. He has only the little fmger and the thumb"

* * *

Mason felt as if he had been driving forever. He rubbed the tiredness out of his eyes and focused again on the narrow strip of black asphalt winding endlessly out of the darkness into the glare of his headlights. He saw the speedometer needle was up over the hundred kilometer mark again and slowed down. He held his wrist down close to the lighted dashboard and looked at his watch. It was just after midnight. He shook his head. Jesus! It seems like I left the main road miles ago and have been driving in this goddamn woods for hours! I must be almost there by now. He pressed down on the accelerator and picked up speed again.

It was more than six hours since he left Naples and he was still trying to figure the whole thing out. He had tried a hundred times on the flight to Strasbourg, then another hundred on the long drive to Bitche. But even now dozens of questions still raced around in his head. He continued to berate himself Stupid! That's what I was, stupid! I should have known better than talk about Molte's whereabouts on the telephone. I should have known someone might be listening He came to his own defense. But Dietz! Jesus Christ! I still can't believe it! All the time we spent together and he was really that guy Rothman who was in the concentration camp with Kopt. Mason shook his head again. The bastard sure had me fooled. And now I've gone and delivered Lisa and her father right into his hands. How stupid could I be! Well, one thing he didn't lie about; there's an old Maginot Line fortress down the end of this road somewhere; the cop in Bitche told me that when he gave me directions. But the whole story about an uncle's having a farm here; that was all bullshit. The cop said there was no farm around here for miles.

The winding road twisted sharply one way then the other. Mason had to slow down. He shook his head. I still don't understand it. What the hell is Kopt up to? If he wanted Molte killed, why didn't he just have Rothman do it in Metz? Wait a minute—maybe Molte's already dead and Kopt is keeping Lisa alive just in case I don't show. He knows I'm on to him now, and that he can't take a chance I'll implicate him in this business with Molte. He knows I won't talk so long as Rothman has Lisa as a hostage. That's why he's gone through all this shit to get me out here, so Rothman can get rid of me. And after that, Rothman is supposed to kill Lisa too. Mason bit his lip.

His hands tightened on the steering wheel as he pressed down on the accelerator.

He was back driving as fast as the winding road would let him. Outside was still nothing but dark woods on both sides. Okay, okay, that all makes sense, he told himself. But why the hell did Kopt pick this place; why have Rothman get me all the way out here where there's nothing but an old Maginot Line fortress, he wondered. He could now feel the cold sweat running down under his arms again. He was wondering about something else too: what a *Shcheeta's* knife was like.

He came up over the crest of a hill and had to hit the brakes. Only a hundred feet ahead the road ended abruptly in a small clearing. Beyond it was nothing but more dark woods. He turned off the motor and the headlights, then let the car coast the rest of the way. When he reached the clearing, he stopped. He opened the door as quietly as he could and got out. He could see he was at the foot of a mountain, all around him nothing but thick dense woods. He listened. The only sound was the wind blowing through the tops of the tall trees. His eyes adjusted to the darkness and he saw, on the other side of the clearing, a narrow slit of light extending a few feet up from the ground. He started cautiously towards it. As he drew nearer, he could see it was coming from an opening in some sort of concrete structure built into the side of the mountain. In front of it was a deep moat, an iron drawbridge leading across to a thick steel door. The door was ajar, the light coming from behind it, inside the structure. He hesitated for a moment at the drawbridge, then crossed it quickly to the door. He stopped and listened. There was no sound coming from inside. He peered through the opening in the door. Behind it a cement passageway went straight back for several yards, then turned sharply out of sight. He took a deep breath, then slipped through the door and started down the passageway. He came to where it turned, stopped and listened again. Still nothing but silence. He kept going. The passageway ended in what looked like the beginning of a subway tunnel. It was dark and dirty, lighted only by a string of bare bulbs hanging from its arched ceiling. Its rough stone floor was bisected by narrow gauge railroad tracks that went straight back into the mountain as far as he could see. He stopped to listen again, and then entered the tunnel, walking slowly, keeping between the tracks and away from the walls laced with thick black electrical cables. He shivered. Outside, it had been a warm summer night; now he was cold and could feel a clammy wetness under his shirt. But it was not just the temperature making him shiver. He was thinking about Rothman waiting up ahead for him. The bastard's in here somewhere, he told himself. But where? He shivered again.

He was only a short distance inside the tunnel when he heard something—a dull throbbing sound coming from somewhere up ahead. The throbbing grew louder as he continued deeper into the tunnel. He stopped. Ahead of him, light was coming from an opening cut into the wall on one side. He approached it slowly. It was a doorway. He could feel his heart beating. Rothman could be waiting for him right there, he thought. He edged up to the light and looked in the doorway. It led into a large concrete room where four huge generators, the size of locomotives, were all pulsating loudly. Except for the generators, the room was empty. He breathed a sigh of relief; it was just the power plant that provided the light and ventilation for the place, he decided.

He continued down the tunnel, pausing every few steps to stop and listen, and peer into the darkness ahead. He was now deep inside the mountain. The tunnel couldn't go on forever, he told himself; it had to lead somewhere. He kept going. He came to a bend in the tunnel and stopped. Ahead of him was a whole section of the tunnel with light coming from doorways on both sides. He could feel his shirt now soaked with sweat. He bit his lip. The bastard could be waiting for me in any one of those doorways. He entered the area slowly, his eyes shifting back and forth, expecting any moment to have Rothman leap out at him. The doorways all led to empty cement rooms. Some were large, with rows of urinals and washbasins, clearly once the barracks of the soldiers stationed in the old fortress. Others, smaller, appeared to have been command posts and communication centers. He kept going, past what he could tell had been the mess hall, the kitchen, a hospital, its cold metal operating table still in the center, a recreation room, its walls still decorated with a faded mural of Snow White and the Seven Dwarfs. There was even a jail. He saw countless other rooms whose purposes he could only guess. All were bare and cell-like, empty and deserted. The whole place gave him the creeps.

He came to the end of the lighted section and entered the dark tunnel again, following the narrow gauge tracks that were taking him deeper and deeper into the mountain. Soon he could no longer see the lighted section back in the tunnel behind him, the only light now coming from the string of bare bulbs hanging from the ceiling He stopped. He thought he had heard something, something that sounded like whispering. He stepped quickly into the shadows and pressed himself up against the wall of the tunnel. He waited, the cold dampness of the cement only inches from his face, listening All he could hear was the faint throbbing of the generators far back in the tunnel behind him.

Suddenly, the lights hanging from the ceiling of the tunnel all went out, and everything was pitch darkness. He heard a click and a flashlight was shined in his face.

"Ah, Mason. We have been waiting for you."

The voice was Kopt's.

* * *

Mason shielded his eyes from the flashlight. "Kopt! So, you're here too. Where's Lisa? And her father? What have you done with them?"

Kopt's voice was calm. "All in good time, Mr. Mason, all in good time. They are both here." His voice hardened. "But do not move. You are helpless in the dark, and I have the only light."

"Where are they, Kopt? If you've—"

"Do not move! Neither has been harmed—yet. Do exactly as I tell you." The light went out and Mason was again in total darkness. He heard Kopt's voice. "Now, listen to me."

"I'm listening, Kopt."

"I am going to shine the light on the floor. As the light moves, follow it. Do you understand?"

"Yeah, I understand."

There was a click, and a spot of light appeared at Mason's feet. It started moving deeper into the tunnel. Mason followed it.

"Good, Mason, good. It is only a short distance now and we will be there."

The spot of light on the floor led Mason through a small doorway. Then it went out, and he was in total darkness again. He waited for Kopt's next instruction. "Now, Mason, feel behind you. There is a chair there. Sit on it."

"Look, Kopt, I don't know what the hell you're—"

"Silence!" There were two quick clicks as Kopt turned his flashlight on, then off again. The interval between the two clicks was enough. Mason gasped. In the brief flash of light he saw Lisa in a wooden chair against the cement wall. Behind her, a man was standing holding a knife at her throat. Then it was pitch darkness again. He heard Kopt's voice, then Lisa's. "Sit down, Mason."

"Please do what he says, Steve."

Mason felt behind him for the chair. He found it and sat down.

Kopt's voice was calm again. "You see, Mason, I hold all the cards. If you are thinking of doing anything foolish, remember that Otto has only to—" He paused. "But I am sure you will not do anything foolish."

For several moments there was silence. Then Mason heard what sounded like mumbling. At first he did not know what it was. Then he realized it was Kopt chanting softly in Hebrew. The chanting stopped and Mason heard Kopt's voice again in the darkness. "You will have to forgive me for savoring this moment, but I have waited more than thirty years for it." His voice paused. "And now, fmally, it has come. So, let us begin." Mason heard the metallic clank of a mechanical switch, and the room was flooded with light. Mason blinked in the sudden brightness. His eyes widened at the bizarre scene before him. He was in a cement room like the ones he had walked past earlier. This one had two doorways: one leading back to the tunnel; the other, a smaller arched one where he could see stone steps going down to a dark chamber below.

Standing by the smaller doorway was Molte, wearing the steel gray uniform of a *Wehrmacht* officer. The uniform did not fit him; it was too big and hung loosely on his thin frame. His arms were at this side and he was staring across the room to where Kopt, dressed in the degrading flannel of a concentration camp inmate, was standing, one hand still resting on the light switch, the other holding his heavy, ivory-knobbed cane. Between the two men, resting on a tripod, was a fully loaded thirty-caliber machine gun, its barrel pointed directly at Molte.

Mason looked at Lisa. Her face was full of anger and defiance. She was bravely ignoring the knife at her throat, her eyes fixed on Molte. The man behind her was Dietz all right. But he wasn't Dietz anymore; he was someone else. The warm friendly face was gone, replaced by a cold expressionless mask. Mason stared at him, trying to picture him as the fun loving engineer he had spent so much time with the past several months. But there was nothing to work with; Dietz was gone; the man he was looking at was a stranger, someone he had never seen before.

Kopt took his hand off the switch and limped into the center of the room. "This leg of mine, it becomes uncomfortable when I do not walk on it." He looked at Mason. "You will remember, the last time we met, my telling you how it was broken many years ago when Otto and I tried to escape from the camp at Mauthausen. And Otto's hand, look at it. He too has his souvenir of those days." He turned to Rothman. "Yes, my loyal friend, those were dark days we spent together back then." He paused. "But tonight, tonight is the night I have promised you all these years." He looked again at Mason. "Yes, I told you about Mauthausen. But there was something I did not tell you. Mauthausen was not the first. Two years before, when I was barely thirteen, I was sent with my father to another place. Yes, another place, worse than Mauthausen, and—" He paused. "Yes, right here in this very fortress." He motioned with his cane around the room. "During the war, this fortress did not fire a single shell. It surrendered without resistance after the Germans had crossed the Meuse." He stood for a moment looking up at the ceiling. "Yes, I know the history of this place well. After it surrendered, it remained empty for a time. Then, in 1941, the Germans reopened it as a prison for captured Russian soldiers." He pointed out toward the tunnel

"The rooms you walked past in the *Caserne* were converted into prison cells." He paused. "There is another tunnel, one you did not see, where there were also cells, smaller ones, in the ammunition *magazin.*" He raised his cane slowly over his head. "The ammunition *magazin!* Ah, that is where the drama we will conclude tonight all began!" He started pacing back and forth again. "While the fortress was being used as a prison for Russian soldiers, the roundup of Jews in Alsace began. The Gestapo wanted a place to interrogate the Jews before shipping them east to the extermination camps. A portion of the fortress was turned over to the Gestapo for that purpose." He paused. "The Commandant of the prison could have prevented this, but did not."

"That is not so!"

Mason and Lisa looked up in surprise as the protest came from Molte. The old man's face was flushed. "If I had tried to interfere—"

Kopt thumped his heavy cane on the floor. "Ah! The beginning of the denouement!"

Molte looked at Lisa. "Yes, it is true I was Commandant of this place during those years. But I swear to you none of the Russian prisoners in my charge were ever mistreated."

"I believe you, Papa, I believe you. I know you would never—" Her words were cut off by the cold blade of Rothman's knife pressing against her throat.

Kopt snarled at Molte. "What about the Jews, ***Herr*** former Commandant? What about the Jews?"

"The Jews were the responsibility of the Gestapo, and the

Gestapo was not under the direction of the army. As Commandant, I insisted that all prisoners, including Jews, be treated humanely. But there were limits to which I could interfere with the Gestapo. If I had interfered too much, I would simply have been replaced. I made certain the Jews had clothing and medical attention and—"

Kopt shook his cane angrily. "But what about food?"

"The Jews were to receive the same as the other prisoners. The allotment was small, but the Jews were to get what the Russians did; those were my orders."

Kopt turned and looked at Lisa. "You did not know that *Herr* Molte was Commandant of a prison camp, did you?"

Lisa glared at him. "I do not know who you are, or why you are doing this. But I know my father is telling the truth when he says—"

"Enough!" Kopt cut her off, and limped back into the center of the room. "Let us continue with the story. The denouement is only beginning."

Molte had been studying Kopt's face. "I do not know you. Is there some reason I should?"

Kopt's loose lips twisted into a smile. "Yes, *Herr* Molte, yes! And before this night is over, you will remember!" For a moment the two men stood glaring at each other. Then Kopt shrugged. "But perhaps I am being premature. Where was I? Oh, yes, the food.

There was not enough food. The Jews in the ammunition ***magazin*** were starving. If the Russians were not being fed any better, they too were starving. The situation in the ***magazin*** became so desperate that talk began of begging the guards for food." Kopt leaned his cane against the cement wall and wiped his forehead with his flannel shirt. "One night, one of the Jews, a Rabbi, broke into the ***paneterie*** and stole three loaves of bread. He was caught and taken before the head of the Gestapo." Kopt turned to Molte. "Do you remember the head of the Gestapo, ***Herr*** Molte?"

"He was a detestable little man; I've forgotten his name." "Weiss."

"Yes, that was it, Weiss."

"And the incident involving the bread, do you remember that? "Only vaguely."

"What do you remember about it? Tell us."

"I remember only that Weiss came to me and said he had caught one of the Jews stealing food."

"Yes, go on."

"He wanted to shoot the Jew as an example to the others." "You talk of one Jew. There were two, were there not?"

Molte thought for a moment. "I can't remember. It was a long time ago."

"Think, ***Herr*** Molte, think!"

"I remember now. The man had a son. Weiss told me he was going to make the son watch the execution."

Kopt limped over to Molte. "The son, ***Herr*** Molte, do you remember him?"

Molte shook his head. "No. It was a long time ago, and—" He stopped, and looked at Kopt.

Kopt nodded his head slowly. "Yes, ***Herr*** Molte, I am that son."

For several moments, neither of them spoke. Then Kopt continued. "But the story is not finished. There is still the most dramatic part to come." He stepped closer to Molte. "Tell me, ***Herr*** Molte, what did you say to Weiss when he came to you that night?"

I protested. I said he should punish the man some other way, that the offense was not serious enough to shoot him."

"And then—?"

"Weiss insisted. He said this particular Jew was a troublemaker." Molte became impatient. "But all of this was long ago. What difference does it make now? Get on with whatever your purpose is here. I have no desire to continue laboring the past with you." He stared defiantly at Kopt.

Kopt turned away from him and limped over to Rothman. He pointed to the knife at Lisa's throat. "Perhaps, Otto, if you would make just a small incision, *Herr* Molte will—"

Molte threw up his hand. "No, stop. I will tell you everything I remember."

Kopt nodded. "Yes, everything, *Herr* Molte."

"Weiss said if I interfered, he would call Berlin and have me transferred."

Kopt sneered. "To the Russian front, I suppose."

Molte did not respond.

"So you agreed?"

"I had no choice. Punishment of the Jews was something I had no authority to interfere with and—"

"No authority to interfere!" Kopt screamed at him. "No authority to interfere!" He pounded his cane on the floor in anger. "Oh, how many of you Germans have used that lame excuse to escape your guilt in the

Holocaust." He shook his fist at Molte. "You, you were the Commandant of the prison. You were the only one who could order a prisoner shot. Tell me if that is not true, *Herr* Molte." "But—"

"But you did not want to risk being sent to the Russian front!" Kopt spit on the floor at Molte's feet. "And you say you were a soldier! You may have worn the uniform of a soldier, but you were no better than those like Weiss with the swastika on their sleeve. You may have deceived the prosecutors at Nuremburg with your protestations about being simply a soldier." He glared at Molte. "But what about here, in this place, when my father's life was at stake, were you a soldier then? Did you say to that snake, Weiss, 'No, I will go to the Russian front before I will allow you to shoot a helpless old man for stealing a few loaves of bread?' No, you did nothing to prevent Weiss from killing my father." Kopt's face was flushed, the sweat pouring down the creases in his flabby jowls. He turned and limped back into the center of the room.

Mason looked at Molte. The old man was pale, his eyes staring down at the floor.

Kopt continued. "I will tell the rest of the story myself. My father and I were brought to this very room. There, where *Herr* Molte is, my father was made to stand, dressed as I am now in these humiliating clothes." He pointed to the small arched doorway. "Down there is what the designers of the fortress called the ***Depot Mortuaire,*** a chamber where the bodies of those killed in battle could be stored until they could receive a decent burial outside. For the French it was a grisly but necessary part of their Maginot Line. For the Gestapo, however, with their diabolical minds, it served quite another purpose. They filled the entire chamber with carbolic acid and—" Kopt wiped his forehead again with his flannel shirt. "Oh, how many Jews spent their last moments on this earth writhing in agony down there!" He glared at Molte. "And it was down there they threw my father's body after—" His voice cracked with emotion. "Look down into the chamber now, ***Herr*** Molte; I have had it filled again with carbolic acid, this time with a special additive from my Hoch laboratories." He limped to the other side of the room. "Here, on this very spot, is where you were standing, near a machine gun like this one, waiting for Weiss to give the order to fire. Do you remember that moment? Think, ***Herr*** Molte, think' We are approaching the grand finale of the denouement!"

Molte lifted his eyes slowly and looked at Kopt. "It was a long time ago. We all make mistakes."

Kopt snarled at him. "I have not forgotten it one day in the forty years that have passed. But there is something else, *Herr* Molte, something important you have left out. Try to remember."

"I remember only that your father said something to you."

Kopt thumped his cane on the floor. "Yes! And that is the key, *Herr* Molte! Just before you gave the order to fire, my father turned and spoke to me in Hebrew. He spoke to me of *zachuth. Zachuth,* a Hebrew word even most Jews do not truly understand. It means the living have it in their power to redeem the souls of the dead. A son, by an act of atonement, can erase the humiliation of his father's death and deliver his father's soul from a judgment in Gehenna. That night, when my father spoke to me in Hebrew, he said, 'Gezar, my son, this man, Molte, is going to have me killed, right in front of your eyes. And there is nothing you can do to prevent it. Accept it. Someday, you will return to this place. You will find this man, Molte, and bring him here. He has a son. You will find the son and bring him here also. Then, on this very spot, you will kill this man, Molte, in front of his son. You will do this, Gezar, and nothing will stop you because it is the act of atonement for which my soul will be crying out ***zachuth! Zachth!'*** Kopt's head dropped on his chest, and for several moments he said nothing. Then he looked up. "Yes, ***Herr*** Molte, it has taken me many years to fulfill the sacred covenant my father gave me that night. But I have finally done it. I have found you and brought you back to this place." He slowly raised the end of his cane. "And I have found your son and brought him here also." He lowered the cane slowly until it was pointing directly at Mason. "Yes, ***Herr*** Molte, this is your son!"

Mason and Lisa both gasped and looked at each other in disbelief. Mason jumped up from his chair, jabbing his finger at Kopt. "You're crazy! You're out of your—"

Kopt shouted at Mason. "Get back in the chair!" He pointed his cane again at the knife Rothman was holding at Lisa's throat. Mason sat down, still glaring at Kopt.

Kopt continued with his story. "Yes, I know you think it impossible. You think your father was killed in an air raid in 1940. That is what you were told, but it was not the truth. When the Germans bombed your city, your father was not there. He had left your mother, and was with the ***Wehrmacht*** in Poland. Is that not so, ***Herr*** Molte?"

Molte remained silent.

Kopt looked again at Mason. "You were born Etienne Molte. After the bombing, your mother took you and fled to the United States where she took her maiden name, LaBouille. She told everyone her husband had been killed in the bombing. It was a convenient story; she was in a new country and no one knew her. You became Etienne LaBouille. Then, when your mother died and the American family adopted you, you became Stephen Mason." Kopt paused and again wiped his forehead with his flannel shirt. "It was not a simple matter to find you. It took many years. Even when I finally found you, I still did not know where your father was. And I had to devise a plan that would bring you both to this remote place." He paused. "A challenging problem, was it not?"

Mason was still stunned by the revelation the Molte was his father. But now he was only half listening to Kopt. His eyes were surveying the room, his brain struggling to think of some way to stop Kopt from what he was going to do. He bit his lip. Maybe, if I pick the right time, I can get to Kopt before—He looked at the sharp blade of Rothman's knife only inches from Lisa's throat. No, that would be crazy; I'd never make it. But time is running out on me; I've got to think of something"

Kopt was still speaking to him. "Yes, it was a challenging problem. Fortunately, I was not without resources. I had money, power and influence, and I used them all. When I discovered you were a lawyer, I devised the plan I needed, and created the HochChimique matter as a cover story." He smiled. "Getting your partner, Templeton, to agree to an undisclosed assignment required a certain degree of diplomacy. And of course I had to be careful that my selection of you rather than one of the others he suggested, did not arouse suspicion. But, in the end, it all went like clockwork. Not once did you suspect the man you knew as Carl Dietz, whom you were being so careful to deceive, was really Otto, engaged in a deeper deception, of which you were the object." Kopt turned to Rothman.

"I congratulate you, my friend; your performance exceeded my highest expectations; it was flawless. And, except for the small part played by that Dutch woman you employed, you did it entirely alone, as I wished. I knew I could count on you." He turned again to Mason. "Only once did you come close to causing me difficulty, in

Wiesbaden when you nearly discovered Otto in the back seat of the Mercedes. That was Sieg's fault; he should not have parked so close to the casino. When the incident was reported to me, I was surprised. Sieg had been with me almost as long as Otto, and I had never known him to be careless before." He paused. "But now it is time to conclude the business that has brought us to this place. I have told the whole story so that all of you, before you die, understand that I have not made this long journey across the years simply for vengeance, but for something beyond vengeance." He leaned his cane against the wall, and knelt down behind the machine gun. He wrapped his hands around the firing grips. "Now, Etienne Molte, son of Hans Molte, watch, as I was made to watch that night long ago when my father was killed in this very place." His fmgers slipped into the spaces in front of the double triggers.

Mason's body tightened, his mind racing to think of something he could do. Kopt leaned forward and sighted down the barrel of the gun. "*Zachuth,* my father, *zachuth.* I now fulfill your sacred covenant and deliver you from—" He stopped. There was a noise outside in the tunnel. They all listened. Footsteps were echoing along the concrete passageway. Someone was coming. They heard him call out.

"Hep! La bas! Police! Qui va la?"

Kopt hissed for everyone to be silent, then motioned to Rothman "A policeman, probably from the local **gendarmerie.** You know what to do."

Rothman, keeping his knife at Lisa's throat, dragged her off the chair and across the room to the doorway. He pressed back against the wall and waited.

The footsteps were just outside the room. Suddenly, a policeman appeared in the doorway. A young man, barely in his twenties, he was carrying a flashlight and a nightstick. He saw the machine gun, dropped the nightstick, and reached for the pistol on his belt. The ***shcheeta*** was on him like a cat. Mason had never seen anyone move so fast. Rothman pushed Lisa to the floor and lunged across the doorway, his knife only a blur flicking under the ***gendarme's*** chin as if brushing something off the collar of his blue uniform. The expression of surprise was still on the young man's face, his forgers still fumbling to open the metal clasp of his holster, when the dark red line began to show on his neck. Starting high behind one ear, it spread quickly down across his throat. Then suddenly it widened and his whole neck opened into a grotesque grinning mouth of blood. He gaped down in horror at the fountain of red spurting out over the front of his uniform. His eyes turned glassy and he fell forward into the pool of blood already on the floor.

Lisa screamed. Mason sprang from his chair, grabbed Kopt's cane and swung it as hard as he could at the metal light switch on the wall. The switch clanked down and the room plunged into darkness. Mason shouted to Molte. "Get out of the way before he fires."

It was too late. Kopt was already squeezing the triggers. The room reverberated with the staccato burst of the machine gun and flames spewed out of the barrel towards where Molte was standing. Mason swung the cane again in the darkness. He felt its heavy ivory knob strike something hard, and the firing stopped. For several moments, everything was quiet. Then Rothman's voice broke the silence. "Gezar? Are you all right? Gezar?" There was no reply. "Gezar, speak to me."

Mason knew it was only a matter of seconds before the *sheheeta* figured out what happened. He groped through the darkness to the wall where he had seen the thick electrical cable. He found the cable, wrapped his fmgers around it, and followed it along the wall to the light switch. He felt around the switch for the metal lever. Damn! The blow from the cane had broken the lever off; all he could feel was a short stub. He tried to move but it wouldn't budge. Behind him, Rothman was calling out again in the darkness. "Gezar? Gezar?"

Mason knew he didn't have a chance against Rothman in the dark. He tried again to move the broken stub. It still wouldn't budge. He dug his fmgers into the switch as far as they would go, got as much of a grip as he could on the broken stub, then lifted with all his strength. The stub moved a little, then snapped up. The room was flooded with light again.

Lisa, still sprawled on the floor where Rothman had thrown her, was looking in horror at what had happened. Molte was dead, his body crumpled against the wall, his ill-fitting uniform riddled with bullet holes. The burst from the machine gun had caught him right in the chest. Kopt's heavy body was draped over the barrel of the gun, his huge bald head crushed like an enormous broken egg, one side of it nothing but a gelatinous mass of blood and brain tissue.

Rothman was standing over the dead *gendarme*. He looked at Kopt, then snarled at Mason. "You son of a bitch! I'm going to cut your balls off for this!" He stepped over the dead **gendarme** and started towards Mason. Mason, still holding Kopt's cane, raised it over his head. The anger in Rothman's face drained into a twisted smile. "Forget it, Mason, you don't stand a chance." Mason could feel the sweat pouring down his back. The bastard's right, he thought; the guy's a professional killer, trained to kill people in situations like this.

Rothman shuffled from one side to the other until he had Mason's back to the small arched doorway; then he moved in closer. Mason backed up, keeping his eye on the sharp blade of the knife Rothman was now rotating slowly in a circle in front of him. Mason could see, over his shoulder, that he was now only a few feet from the top of the stone steps leading down to the dark chamber. This is it, he told himself; the bastard's got me cornered; I can't back up any more. He'll make a lunge and that'll be it. And he's too quick for me; I've seen that. Even with Kopt's cane, I'm no match for him. The only chance I've got is if I can pick the time...if I can make him lunge when I want him to...then maybe...maybe...just maybe...

He kept poking the cane in Rothman's face, trying to keep him from coming any closer. Rothman just sneered. "It's no use, Mason,

I'm too good at this." He face twisted into a crooked smile "And when I'm finished with you, I'm going to slit the throat of your girlfriend over there." He moved closer, rotating his knife in smaller, more menacing, circles. But now, it was not his knife that Mason was watching; he was keeping his eye on something else: Rothman's back foot. He stopped poking the cane at Rothman, and raised it over his head again. Rothman hesitated, then took a step forward. Mason's body tightened. Okay, fella, this is it! He swung the cane, appeared to lose his grip on it, and let it slip out of his hands. As it fell to the floor, he reached out to grab it. It was a dangerous gamble. For the first time, he was putting himself within reach of the ***shcheeta's*** knife. Rothman took the bait and lunged, his long blade going for Mason's throat. But now Mason was moving too. Already down low reaching for the fallen cane, he grabbed Rothman's extended arm, and spun is fast under it. He snapped the arm over his shoulder and swept his leg back as high as he could in an arabesque. His leg caught the inside of Rothman's thigh in a perfect ***uchi mata.*** As Rothman flew over his shoulder, Mason let go of his arm. The ***shcheeta*** cart wheeled through the arched doorway and tumbled down the stone steps. Mason heard him splash into darkness below.

Lisa jumped up, grabbed the dead *gendarme's* flashlight, and rushed over to where Mason was standing. They could hear Rothman screaming Mason took the flashlight and shined it down into the dark chamber. At the end of the beam of light they could see Rothman.

He was flailing his arms frantically in a pool of bubbling yellow liquid, trying to lift himself out of it. All around him were glistening silver crystals hissing loudly and sending a pungent smell up the steps. The smell was so pungent Mason and Lisa had to turn away. The screaming stopped, and they looked again. The yellow liquid was bubbling violently now. Rothman had disappeared into it. Lisa ran to where Molte was lying crumpled against the wall. She knelt on the floor, lifted his limp body up, and cradled it in her arms. She began sobbing.

Mason, holding one hand over his nose and mouth, kept the flashlight pointed down into the dark chamber. The chemical reaction was now at its most violent; the whole chamber a bubbling cauldron. Rothman reappeared, his face and arms horribly eaten away by the carbolic acid. Now barely recognizable as a human being, he slowly sank back into the boiling liquid again. For several minutes, the chemical reaction continued. Then slowly it subsided; the crystals stopped hissing; the yellow liquid returned to quiescence.

* * *

Mason could tell it was going to be another hot day. The sun was not yet up and already the air was warm and sticky. He was standing with Lisa at the edge of the clearing, now filled with police cars and ambulances. Through the thick trees he could see the pink glow of the false dawn. All around him the woods were coming alive with the sounds of birds beginning their day. He watched the last stretcher being carried out of the fortress to a waiting ambulance. Like the two before, it was covered with a blanket and he could not tell whose body it was. He saw Lisa was crying. He took her in his arms and held her tightly. He watched over her shoulder as the three ambulances drove away in single file up the hill toward Bitche.

One of the ***gendarmes*** approached them. He saluted, then spoke to them in English. "I am Captain Delmas. The young policeman who was killed here last night had called the ***gendarmerie*** before he went into the fortress. He said he had heard rumors of people going into the fortress and, when you stopped to ask directions about it yesterday, he decided to follow you and investigate. We told him not to go into the fortress until we arrived. But regrettably—" He paused. "In any event, I must ask you both to come to the ***gendarmerie*** and provide statements. I will see that you are not detained any longer than absolutely necessary." He paused, then turned to Lisa. His voice softened. "I understand that the man killed by the machine gun was your father?"

Lisa hesitated. "Well, he was really—"

Mason answered for her. "He was really the father of both of us."

Lisa smiled and squeezed Mason's hand.

Delmas frowned briefly at Mason's answer, then continued. "His body is being brought to the morgue in Bitche. The people there will assist you with whatever burial arrangements you wish to make."

Lisa looked up at Mason. "Steve, if it's all right with you, I would like Papa to be buried in the cemetery at Saint Avoid. It is a military cemetery not far from Metz where both French and German soldiers are buried. I remember Papa taking me there once and telling me how nice he thought it was that soldiers from both sides could be buried together."

Mason squeezed her hand. "I agree. I think that's just the right place."

Delmas walked with them to Mason's car and waited while they got in. He leaned down at the window. His voice was still soft. "I know this has been a terrible night for both of you." He stepped back, saluted; then he walked to the police car and got in. The red light on the roof of the police car began rotating.

Mason turned his car around and started to leave. He stopped to take one last look at the old fortress. Two *gendarmes* were putting up a wooden barricade across the iron bridge leading across the moat to the heavy steel door. His thoughts went back to that snowy Monday morning in Boston when he met with Templeton and first heard the name Kopt. He shook his head. It all seemed like ages ago. He saw that Lisa, too, was looking out the window. She was not crying anymore. He reached over, took her hand in his, and squeezed it. She smiled at him. He took his fmger and ran it around the top of his ear. "Do you know what I'm thinking right now?"

Lisa was still smiling "No, what, Steve?"

He laughed. "I'm wondering what you're going to order for both of us at dinner our first night on the Isle of Capri."

* * *